"You could use a few lessons in romantic techniques, Mr. Roman. Women do not like to be manhandled," Hannah said smoothly.

He pulled her tight against his chest. "What do they like, Hannah?"

Strength and power, she thought as she looked up at him. Even the arrogance he wore like a merit badge attracted her. The sense of danger that hovered over him was a powerful aphrodisiac. All the things he was—bold and brash and wild and ruthless—reminded her of Alaska, the land that had held her captive for years.

She put on her most fetching smile, then looked into his eyes and lied. "We like to be asked."

"Then, Miss Hannah Donovan, I'm asking politely. May I kiss you?"

"No."

His mouth descended on hers with the swiftness of the eagles she'd seen attacking their quarry. Her blood grew hot with the fever of challenge. She gave back as good as she got and had the satisfaction of feeling his sharp intake of breath as she moved brazenly against him.

His arms tightened and his mouth ravaged hers in a fierce sort of hunger. A fever began to build in her blood, as she felt her control slipping. Finally she pulled away. "I said no."

"But your eyes said yes. You're a torrid woman, Hannah. . . ."

WHAT ARE *LOVESWEPT* ROMANCES?

They are stories of true romance and touching emotion. We believe those two very important ingredients are constants in our highly sensual and very believable stories in the *LOVESWEPT* line. Our goal is to give you, the reader, stories of consistently high quality that may sometimes make you laugh, sometimes make you cry, but are always fresh and creative and contain many delightful surprises within their pages.

Most romance fans read an enormous number of books. Those they truly love, they keep. Others may be traded with friends and soon forgotten. We hope that each *LOVESWEPT* romance will be a treasure—a "keeper." We will always try to publish

LOVE STORIES YOU'LL NEVER FORGET
BY AUTHORS YOU'LL ALWAYS REMEMBER

The Editors

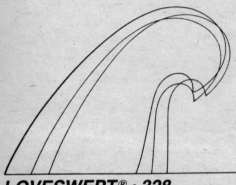

LOVESWEPT® • 328

Peggy Webb
Any Thursday

BANTAM BOOKS
TORONTO • NEW YORK • LONDON • SYDNEY • AUCKLAND

ANY THURSDAY
A Bantam Book / May 1989

If you would be interested in receiving protective vinyl
covers for your Loveswept books, please write to this address
for information:

Loveswept
Bantam Books
P.O. Box 985
Hicksville, NY 11802

ISBN 0-553-21994-4

Published simultaneously in the United States and Canada

Bantam Books are published by Bantam Books, a division
of Bantam Doubleday Dell Publishing Group, Inc. Its trademark, consisting of the words "Bantam Books" and the
portrayal of a rooster, is Registered in U.S. Patent and
Trademark Office and in other countries. Marca Registrada.
Bantam Books, 666 Fifth Avenue, New York, New York 10103.

PRINTED IN THE UNITED STATES OF AMERICA

O   0 9 8 7 6 5 4 3 2 1

For Shirley and Jack
—my cousins, my friends
—who know a little about Alaska and a lot about love

One

He missed the noise. He missed the hustle and bustle. He even missed the smog. Jim Roman had landed in Greenville, Mississippi, exactly forty-five minutes earlier, and already he felt the need to be back in San Francisco. He was like an addict, he thought. The big city gave him his fix.

It was only May, but it was hot as hell. He flipped a switch on the dashboard of the car, the one that said air-conditioning, but wasn't surprised that nothing happened. When he rolled the window down, he could hear the ominous clinking and clanging that indicated his rented car probably wouldn't make it over the next hill, let alone to the Donovan spread.

Swearing and sweating, he nursed the car along. Three miles down the road, it shuddered and drew its last breath. He got out and lifted the hood, although he didn't have high hopes of repairing anything. He'd never been good at mechanics.

He jiggled a few wires that looked loose and gave the battery cable a smart tap with a rock he'd picked up from the road. Nothing happened except that he got grease on his hands. He surveyed his surroundings. There was nothing but green pasture as far as the eye could see. It was great country if you were a cow, but he had his heart set on finding a telephone. At that moment he'd be willing to bet that nobody for miles had ever heard of Alexander Graham Bell. He'd often read of the backside of nowhere, and now he was there.

He mopped his face with his handkerchief, then pulled a hand-drawn map from his hip pocket and calculated how far he was from his destination. Five or six miles, he thought. Maybe he could walk it if his loafers would hold out.

"I'll get you for this, John Searles." With a muttered oath he set off down the road.

Hannah Donovan raised her .300 Magnum to her shoulder and sighted along the barrel. The shot cracked in the still air as she picked off a soup can. She pulled the bolt back, shucked the spent shell, and fired again. Another can bit the dust. Handling her bolt-action rifle with expert ease, she got off another three shots in rapid succession.

Suddenly she felt movement beside her legs. The husky that had been sitting at her feet whirled around and raced across the pasture. He was a blur of gray as he leapt into the air and brought down his quarry, a man about the size of a half-grown grizzly.

"Hold him, Pete." She raced behind her dog, arriving only seconds after the big man had hit the ground. She planted her right foot on his chest and pointed her gun at his crotch. "You're trespassing."

The man on the ground chuckled. "You shoot trespassers around here?"

When he laughed, she instinctively knew he was harmless, but a longtime habit of caution kept her hand on the gun. "Only if provoked."

"They told me all about southern hospitality. I never expected to encounter *Miami Vice*. Do you mind pointing that gun somewhere else? I'm partial to that part of my anatomy."

Still holding her gun against him, Hannah looked at her captive. He was big and rugged and handsome, if you liked the dangerous, slightly scarred type. His nose looked as if it had been broken at least once, and there was a faint scar that began in the part of his auburn hair and angled down to his eyebrows. The cleft in his chin saved him from being formidable—that, and his lips. They were sensuous and knowing. They looked as if they would kiss a women so that she'd know she'd been kissed.

She found herself staring at his lips.

"See anything you like?"

She could have shot him. "What are you doing on this property?"

"Do you mind telling Old Yeller to get his fangs out of my face? I can't think while I'm staring at death."

"Pete, sit."

The low-throated growling stopped, and the dog she'd called Pete sat down beside her as docile as a lamb.

"Nice. You must be from *Wild Kingdom*."

Hannah bit back her laughter. It wouldn't do to let this fast-talking stranger get the upper hand. Nobody ever got the upper hand with her, and she wasn't about to let that change now.

The man started to sit up, but she nudged him in the crotch with the gun. "It's loaded."

He quirked his eyebrows. "I always keep it loaded. It comes in handy sometimes."

Hannah's merriment spilled over. She threw back her head and laughed until tears rolled down her cheeks. She unbreached her gun, then leaned down to offer her hand.

"Any man with your sense of humor can't be all bad."

Ignoring her outstretched hand, he propped his arms behind his head and grinned up at her. "I'm not sure I trust you, Annie Oakley."

"I'm not sure you should. I'm a crack shot, and my dog Pete will go for the jugular if I give the command."

"Sounds as though I'm a hell of a lucky guy to still be alive. Is everybody in Greenville like you?"

She grinned. "No. Some are worse."

"My cup runneth over." He sat up and eyed her dog. "What's dog language for 'I'm friendly, don't bite?' "

"You're safe as long as you behave."

He studied her from top to bottom, taking his time. Hannah found his gaze maddening.

"You make a man want to misbehave."

"Don't. I'd hate to have to use this rifle."

"It happens every day on the streets of San Francisco."

"You're from San Francisco?"

"Yes. The name's Jim Roman."

"The syndicated columnist?" The famous investigative reporter, she thought. She'd read his column. He was a hard-hitting, ruthless crusader against crime and corruption. The West Coast Warrior he was called.

"One and the same."

When he stood up, he towered over Hannah, which was not an easy feat. At five-ten she looked most men straight in the eye. She tipped her head back so she could look into his eyes. They were the warm brown of a teddy bear's fur, and right now they were bright with amusement.

"I do apologize for accosting you with the gun. Where I live, dealing with poachers is an everyday occurrence. Pete and I act on reflex."

"Apology accepted." He reached out and pulled her into his chest with a swiftness that caught her off balance. Pete remained seated, but his hackles went up. "I act on reflex too." He tightened his hold so that she could feel the steady hammering of his heart against her T-shirt. His left hand cupped her face. "Now, suppose you tell me why a beautiful woman goes around pointing guns at friendly strangers."

Her dog growled. "Stay, Pete." She gave him the command in a soft voice. Jim Roman didn't intimidate her: He challenged her. She hadn't been challenged in a long, long time. "*Are* you friendly?"

"When it suits me." His fingers brushed across her lips. "And it suits me now."

His mouth came down on hers. The kiss was hard, demanding, and very expert. Hannah was shocked at the quick surge of desire that pulsed through her. She hadn't been so aroused since before she broke off her affair with Dr. Rai Ghayami five years earlier. She'd have to be careful around this man, she decided. She nearly had let her passion for Rai ruin her. It had threatened her independence and her career. She'd vowed that it would never happen again.

Jim Roman ended the kiss as swiftly as he'd begun it. Hannah fought for the control that she prided herself on having.

"If that was meant as a demonstration of your friendliness, I'll have to tell you, Jim Roman—I've had better."

"I never let a challenge go unanswered."

Those expert, knowing lips were on hers again. She felt as if she'd been caught in the middle of one of the sudden storms that lashed Glacier Bay. She felt the raw power of the man, the brute strength, the violence, carefully leashed. And she felt the threat.

When it was over, she had to take a deep breath to get enough oxygen into her starved system.

"Nice, but personally I find whale watching much more interesting."

Jim Roman roared with laughter. "A Siberian husky and a .300 Magnum rifle. I don't doubt for a minute that a woman of your talents has a whale in this cow pasture."

"This cow pasture happens to be Donovan property, and you're still trespassing."

"That's the first good news I've had all day."

"That you're trespassing?"

"That I'm on Donovan property. My rented car broke down about a mile up the road, and I thought I'd take a shortcut through this pasture. I'm looking for Anna Donovan."

"Anna is my mother, and I can assure you that she has no criminal connections. If you mentioned Mafia to her, she'd think it was a new recipe for Italian cake. What possible business can you have with my mother?"

"Then you must be . . ." He paused, searching his

memory for what John Searles, his publisher, had told him. "Hallie? Don't tell me I've besmirched the honor of the bride-to-be?"

"No. Hannah. Hallie and I are twins. You can rest easy. A kiss is the same in the South as it is in San Francisco, of very little consequence. As for besmirching anybody's honor—you'll get no chance."

Hannah slung her gun over her shoulder with unnecessary vigor. She didn't have all day to stand in the pasture and play words game with this outrageous man. She'd come all the way from Alaska to see that her sister's wedding was handled properly, and she had things to do. Besides, the sooner she was out of Jim Roman's company, the better.

"Another challenge, Hannah Donovan?" His voice was deceptively soft. She didn't miss the flame that lit the center of his eyes or the determined set of his jaw.

"A warning, Jim Roman. Hallie's wedding is a time of celebration for all the Donovans. I won't let you or anyone else spoil it."

"My intent is not to spoil the wedding but to report it."

That news didn't surprise Hannah. Her sister was marrying one of America's wealthiest men. Whatever Josh Butler did made news. The only surprise was that Jim Roman was covering the wedding. It was certainly a departure from his usual work. "And your business with my mother?"

"She and my mother are old friends." His hand snaked out and firmly gripped her chin. "As for besmirching your honor . . . that remains to be seen."

Tiny charges of power pulsed through his fingertips to her chin, but she'd be damned if she'd back off. "Remove your hand."

Keeping a firm grip on her chin, he chuckled. "You like to give orders, don't you?"

"Yes."

"Be warned, Hannah. I seldom take them." He let his fingers play over her lips before he released her. "And now, would you mind leading me across this cow pasture to the Donovan house?"

"You say your car is only a mile away?"

"Yes."

"We're five miles from the house, and I have no intention of being in your company any longer than I have to. Show me where your car is, and I'll fix it so you can be on your way."

"You'll fix it?" He snapped his fingers. "Just like that?"

"Precisely. I'm a self-sufficient woman."

"Frankly, I prefer soft and pliant women, but I suppose an independent, bossy woman would come in handy for such things as overhauling the car and repairing the television."

"You're an irritating, arrogant jackass."

"I try."

"Lead me to your car before I change my mind about shooting you."

The car was less than a mile away, just over the rise in the pasture. Jim Roman led the way, apparently paying Hannah Donovan no attention at all. In fact, he was watching her with the trained eye of a man who sees everything and understands most of what he sees. What he saw fascinated him. She was the most beautiful woman he'd ever met. With that dark glossy mane of hair and those clear blue eyes and a body that had been shaped to drive men mad, she looked as if she belonged on the movie screen.

A maverick breeze lifted her glorious hair away from her face. Jim appreciated the sight in silence. Hannah Donovan easily could be his dream woman, except for one thing, her damned independence. His ideal woman would be luscious like her, but she'd be content to keep his home neat and his bed warm. He couldn't imagine Hannah mopping floors and ironing shirts. The man who asked her probably would get a bucket of water over his head and his shirts stuffed down his throat.

When they came to the rented car, he leaned casually against the hood. "Be my guest."

To his amusement, she tackled the mysteries under the hood as if she'd been born with a wrench in her hand.

"Nothing much wrong except this little thingamajig here."

His smile broadened at the sight of her trim little rear as she bent over. Greenville was looking better every minute. He'd raised hell with John Searles about coming, but it seemed there could be compensations. Hannah Donovon, for one. If he was any judge of women—and he was if his track record proved anything—there was quite a hellcat lurking under that independent exterior.

Taming the little wildcat was going to be fun. It was exactly what he needed to pass the time until he could get back to the only thing that stirred his blood—fighting crime in the back alleys and waterfront bars of San Francisco by reporting on it.

"All finished." She glanced up from the hood.

"You have grease."

She put her hand to her face and smeared some on her chin. "Where?"

"Here." He smiled to himself, and with practiced ease kissed her. She fought. Her lean, lithe body bucked against him, and she tried to keep her mouth set. But the passion was there. He could feel it simmering just beneath the surface of her cool exterior. His own body surged in response.

"We're going to be good together, Hannah Donovan."

She backed off and wiped her hand across her mouth. Her expression was filled with fury.

"Not till hell freezes over."

He laughed. "You'd be surprised how fast I can make hell freeze over." He climbed into his rented car and leaned out the window. "Give you a lift, Hannah?"

"I wouldn't ride with you five inches, let alone five miles."

"We'll ride together, Hannah. I promise you that."

His brow rose in a way that made her think of the devil, then he set off toward the Donovan house. She hoped he took a wrong turn and ended up in the Mississippi River.

"Damned arrogant barbarian." Pete's ears perked up at the tone of her voice. She bent over and hugged him. "Not you, old friend. Jim Roman. Ride, indeed." Her cheeks grew hot. She knew full well he hadn't been talking about cars or horses. Excitement stirred deep inside her. The West Coast Warrior wore power and danger like a cloak. She was intrigued, challenged. And also wary. Even though it had been five years since Rai, she remembered what it was like to let priorities slip away, to become so wrapped up in a man, her work became perfunctory and merely adequate.

They'd met in Sri Lanka. He was a cetologist. Both

had been assigned to the research vessel *Glory*, charged with studying a large pod of sperm whales. They'd fallen for each other, hard and fast, and it quickly had gotten out of hand. Her work began to suffer. She had been aware of what was happening but was helpless to change it. With Rai, she'd lost her perspective and her ability to reason. In retrospect, she'd blamed the mystery and beauty of the Indian Ocean, the marvel of their shared work, the glory of their shared passion—anything except herself.

She'd gotten out before it was too late. Putting an ocean between them, she'd devoted herself to her beloved profession, restored her own confidence in her work. And she'd guarded against letting another Rai into her life.

She crossed the ditch that separated the gravel road from the Donovan pasture. Her pulse was still racing from Jim Roman's remark about riding and the images it had evoked.

"I'll probably rue the day I had my opportunity to shoot him and didn't," she muttered.

Hannah found her mother in the kitchen, up to her elbows in petit fours and cheese straws and finger sandwiches. Anna turned at the sound of the back screen door banging shut.

"I declare, Hannah. If you don't do something about Agnes, I'm going to go stark raving crazy. She thinks she knows more about weddings than Amy Vanderbilt. You're the only one in the family who can handle her. She's in the library now, thinking up mischief. If she says we need Italian bowknots one more time, I'm going to—" Abruptly she stopped talking and reached up to wipe away a big spot of grease from Hannah's cheek. She gave her daughter a cagey smile. "Let's forget about this wedding for a while and talk. Just the two of us. It seems I never get to talk to you, with you up there in Alaska doing all that whale research."

Hannah picked up a cheese straw and popped it into her mouth. She smiled at the emphasis her mother put on whale research. Although Anna Donovan would never presume to tell her children what to do, her greatest desire was that they all marry and have big families and live happily ever after—just the way she had with Hannah's father, Matthew.

"Yes, let's talk, Mom."

Taking her mother's hand, Hannah led her to a chair and sat down beside her at the kitchen table. No, she thought, Anna never would say outright what she was thinking, but she'd drop hints that were big enough to fell an elephant.

"Now . . . tell me about Aunt Agnes's latest plan."

Anna pushed an errant pin into her neat salt-and-pepper French twist. "That can wait. Tell me what took you so long out in the pasture. I thought you were just going out for a little target practice."

"I got sidetracked—by Jim Roman. What in hell is he doing in Greenville?"

"Hannah! Watch your language. I declare, I don't know where you get that talk, your brother Paul being a preacher and all. It's enough to scare any man off. Why . . . how in the world did you get sidetracked by Jim Roman?"

"His car broke down, and I fixed it."

"Oh. Is that all?"

Hannah chuckled at the crestfallen look on her

mother's face. "Don't start putting one and one together and getting six."

"Who? Me?"

"Yes, you. I know what you're up to, Mom. And it
won't work. You'll just have to be satisfied that you
raised one daughter who's content to be an old maid."

"Pshaw! You're always teasing me. Just like your
father. He's a nice man, don't you think?"

Hannah grinned. "Pop? I've always thought so."

"There you go, teasing again. Of course your father is wonderful. That's a given. I'm talking about
Jim Roman."

"What I think about Jim Roman won't do to tell in
polite company. How do you know him, Mom?" Jim
had told her, but she wanted to hear it from her
mother. She figured he wasn't above lying to get
what he wanted.

"He's the son of my college roommate and one of
my best friends, Mary Louise Pritikin. You remember Mary Louise, don't you?"

Hannah laughed. Her mother had so many people
she called best friends, it would take the census
bureau to keep up with them all. "No, Mom, I don't.
That was before my time, remember?"

"I forget. My, my, it seems like yesterday—me and
Mary Louise getting our first pair of silk stockings
together." Her face became dreamy as she thought
of old times. "Anyway, she married and moved off to
California, but we've kept in touch over the years. I
still have the card she sent me when Jim was born.
She sent me a card when he got his big, fancy job
too. He writes for that paper . . . what's it called?"

The Daily Spectator." Hannah smiled at her mother's perception of Jim Roman's work. "Writes for

that paper" didn't touch the scope and influence of Jim's column. "I still don't see what he's doing here. Surely *The Daily Spectator* isn't interested in covering a wedding."

"Mary Louise told me he works for a John Searles, who is head of what's called a publishing empire. Isn't that a silly name for a few newspapers and magazines? An empire. Makes me think of the Queen of England."

"Mom . . ."

"I know." Anna held up her hand. "You want me to get to the point. I declare, Hannah. You were always the impatient one. I remember that time Reverend Clemstattler dragged his sermon out so long. You stood up on the back pew and yelled, 'Amen, now let's go home.' "

They laughed together. Then, Hannah, as impatient as ever, gently urged her mother back on the subject.

"Well, you see, Jim Roman is going to write about your sister's wedding for one of those magazines, *America's Elite.* Isn't that nice? I think Tanner's wedding was written about in there too. My, my. Two of my children making big news. And both of them happy as pigs in the sunshine. Did you know Amanda's pregnant again? She and Tanner are not letting any grass grow under their feet. Making up for lost time, they say."

"I didn't know. That's wonderful, Mom. They both want a big family."

"Somebody shot at Jim Roman."

"What?" Hannah was accustomed to her mother's way of dropping one subject and plunging into another. She thought of the rifle she'd hung on the rack on the back porch and wondered what Jim Roman had told her mother about their encounter.

"In San Francisco. That's why Mr. Searles sent him to Greenville. Mary Louise called last night and told me the whole story. I don't think Jim Roman ordinarily writes about weddings, does he?"

"No, Mom. He covers the crime scene."

"Some name that sounds like an Italian cake. That's who's after him. Poor man. I told him he could stay here."

"Here? In this house?" Hannah jumped up and went to the kitchen window. Sure enough, Jim's dusty rented car was parked in their front yard.

"Of course. Would I turn away the son of my best friend, especially after she called and asked me to watch after him? She's had a hard life, and Jim is all she has."

"What about the wedding, Mom? You're swamped as it is. I don't see how we can have another guest in this house. Especially an outsider." Even as she reasoned, Hannah knew it was useless. Her mother had a heart big enough to take in everybody who knocked on the front door, and she also had a stubborn streak. Hannah could see her mind already was made up.

"The son of a friend is never an outsider, and we have plenty of room. Tanner and Amanda and their two girls will be staying in her house in Greenville. Paul and Martie and their children will be here, but your brother Jacob will be the Lord only knows where. I've put Jim in Jacob's room. Right next door to yours."

Hannah sat back down with a plop. She'd known she'd have to deal with her bossy Aunt Agnes; she hadn't counted on having to deal with the West Coast Warrior.

Two

When Hannah left the kitchen, she went straight to the library to deal with Aunt Agnes.

As she pushed open the door, she saw Agnes, her back ramrod straight, her lips pursed, running her finger over a Victorian table.

"Checking for dust, Aunt Agnes?"

Agnes jerked her head around at the sound of Hannah's voice. Hannah always was taken aback that Agnes was so like her brother Matthew in looks and so unlike him in personality. Both were tall and slim with an elegant bearing that spoke of royalty in their lineage. And both had the bright blue eyes of the Black Irish. While Matthew was good-natured and easygoing, Agnes had the disposition of a prickly pear.

"Hannah, you always did have the habit of sneaking up on people. I guess you learned it up there in the frozen wilderness, having to sneak around so polar bears won't eat you up."

"Don't change the subject, Aunt Agnes. The library's clean. I dusted it myself."

"Then you missed a spot." She took a big swipe at the table and held up her hand. "There, see it? If Anna's going to have the wedding reception here instead of at the country club, where all the Presbyterians and Episcopalians go, then I'm bound and determined to see that she does it right. After all, Hallie is my only brother's child, and my favorite niece to boot."

She narrowed her eyes, obviously calculating the effect of her last statement on Hannah. Hannah laughed.

"So you've always said, Aunt Agnes."

"Lord, child, you know I'm just kidding you. I love all of you like you're my own. But I don't see how we're ever going to get you to the altar till you change your ways. Thirty's mighty old not to be married."

"I'm not altar bound, Aunt Agnes. But Hallie is." She crossed the library and took her aunt's arm. "Let's make a pact. Let's work together to make Mom's job easier instead of aggravating her with suggestions. You know she's going to run this wedding exactly as she pleases anyhow."

"Well, I guess if we're not going to the country club, that's all right. But it does appear to me that since Anna's insisting on fixing everything herself instead of having it catered, she could serve Italian bowknots. They're the latest thing in finger foods, you know. Italian bowknots. I read about them in *Redbook*."

"It you want Italian bowknots, Aunt Agnes, I'll see that they're served. But Mom doesn't have time to make them. You have to."

"You know I can't cook worth a flitter."

Hannah knew it was true. "I'll come over to your house and help you, Aunt Agnes." She'd just made the supreme sacrifice. Her cooking was on a par with Aunt Agnes's, but she'd do anything to make this wedding run smoothly.

"That's fine with me. But don't you bring that wolfhound of yours. Your uncle Charlie's allergic to dog hairs."

"Pete's a Siberian husky."

"Husky, smushky. It appears to me that's one of the major reasons you're an old maid. Keeping company with nothing but dogs and whales." Agnes gathered up her hat, a dashing straw bowler, and set it on her head at a jaunty angle. Hannah was reminded of the way Hallie wore her Stetson. "I'll see you this afternoon at four, and don't you dare be late." With that final order, Aunt Agnes swept from the library.

As soon as the door was shut, Hannah picked up the first thing she could get her hands on, a fat book of Eudora Welty's collected stories, and flung it across the room.

"Hell's bells." The book sailed across the back of the sofa and landed with a satisfying plop on the hearth.

"Temper, temper, my dear. Is that any way to catch a husband?" Jim Roman's head appeared over the back of the sofa, then his broad shoulders, then his impressive chest. "You almost beheaded me."

"Pity I didn't. How long have you been back there eavesdropping?"

"Long enough to know that Aunt Agnes considers you to be doomed to oldmaidhood. That's a quaint term. I never hear it on the West Coast. It must be a southern expression."

"We have a lot of things in the South you've never heard of. Manners, for one thing. The very idea, lying on the sofa eavesdropping."

"Actually I was napping until you and Aunt Agnes got into that interesting discussion about Italian bowknots and old maids and wedding receptions. Your charming mother told me to make myself at home. I was looking for a book to read, and all this bucolic peace and quiet put me to sleep." Jim Roman unfolded his long legs and stood up. Picking up the book she'd thrown, he started toward her.

"Don't come any closer," Hannah's hand closed around a brass candlestick. Jim merely laughed and kept on coming.

His lazy grin and relaxed manner almost made Hannah forget his transgressions. But they were many, and she was determined to deal with them.

"Mr. Roman—"

"Call me Jim," he interrupted her smoothly. "After all we've been to each other, don't you think mister is a little too formal?"

"All you've been to me is a pain in the—"

"Association with polar bears has made you testy, Hannah. I have to agree with Aunt Agnes. Unless you mend your ways, you'll never make it to the altar. A sharp tongue, my dear, is a definite obstacle to romance." In three quick strides he was beside her. His hand snaked out and closed over Hannah's, just as she was hefting the candlestick aloft.

Hannah tried to jerk her hand free. But as strong as she was, she was no match for Jim. If she couldn't win the physical battle, she was determined to win the verbal one. "You could use a few lessons in romantic techniques yourself. Women don't like to be manhandled."

He took the candlestick from her hand and pulled her tight against his chest. "What do they like, Hannah?"

Strength and power, she thought as she looked up at him. Even the arrogance he wore like a merit badge attracted her. The sense of danger that hovered over him was a powerful aphrodisiac. All the things he was—bold and brash and wild and ruthless—reminded her of Alaska, the land that had held her captive for years. But she was a willing captive of Alaska's; she would never be a willing captive of Jim Roman's.

Putting on her most fetching smile, she looked into his eyes and lied. "We like to be asked."

"Then, Miss Hannah Donovan, I'm asking politely. May I kiss you?"

"No."

His lips descended on hers with the swiftness of the eagles she'd seen attacking their quarry. She gave back as much as she got. When she finished with him, he'd know he wasn't dealing with any lily-white, trembling maiden.

She twined her hands in his hair, fitted herself brazenly against him. She had the satisfaction of feeling his sharp intake of breath as her tongue boldly explored his mouth.

His arms tightened, and his mouth ravaged hers with a fierce hunger. A fever began to build in Hannah's blood, and she felt her control slipping.

This time it was she who pulled away. Her blue eyes were bright with laughter as she looked up at him.

"I told you no."

"Your eyes said yes." Jim released her and took a step backward. Hannah liked to think of it as a retreat. "You're a torrid woman, Hannah."

"I try . . . but only when it suits me."

"An intriguing woman," Jim continued, dismissing her last remark as if she'd never made it. "What makes a woman like you bury herself in Glacier Bay?" He leaned casually against the back of the sofa, his gaze almost insolent as it swept her from head to toe. "Dr. Hannah Donovan, marine biologist, head of the North Pacific Institute of Oceanographic Research. Two years in Sri Lanka studying sperm and blue whales, one in the rugged, remote Kenai Fjords of Alaska charting the humpback whale, and the last three in Glacier Bay. Raises huskies and competes in the Yukon Quest for recreation. No romantic entanglements." He quirked a sardonic eyebrow upward. "Have I missed anything?"

"I don't do windows."

"I guessed as much."

"Who told you? Mom?"

"A good reporter never reveals his sources." He chuckled. "But I'll have to admit that this source makes the best gingerbread I've ever tasted."

Hannah circled him, giving him the same frank once-over he'd given her. "Jim Roman, the West Coast Warrior, winner of the Pulitzer Prize for a newspaper series on the gang wars that shook the streets of San Francisco a few years back. Knifed twice in the line of duty, the recipient of one car bomb, and most recently the target of the Mafia."

"Your facts are wrong. A good reporter always gets his facts straight."

"Would you care to elaborate?"

"No."

"Then allow me to create a scenario. Famous reporter flees San Francisco, leads the Mafia straight to Greenville and the innocent Donovan family."

"Your family is in no danger." His expression was serious. "Believe me, Hannah. Everybody assumes the Mafia is responsible any time a bullet is fired. We don't know who's after me. We've made some educated guesses, of course. If I had my choice, I'd still be in San Francisco. John Searles took that decision out of my hands. He thinks it best that I keep a low profile for a while."

"If the Mafia is not after you, who in the world mentioned it to my mother?"

"Probably Aunt Agnes. She seems to be the authority on everything."

"What are you working on now, Jim? Who *is* shooting at you?"

He grinned. "You're the only one who has tried it lately."

"I should have pulled the trigger."

"Think of all the fun you'd have missed, Dr. Donovan."

"It boggles the mind, Mr. Roman."

They were facing each other now, squared off like two championship boxers. They both thrived on challenge and battle—Jim against the evil man does in society, and Hannah against the evil man does in nature. The air between them fairly sizzled. Unconsciously Jim braced against the sofa and Hannah ran a hand around the neck of her T-shirt to release the heat.

When the silence between them had stretched almost to the breaking point, Jim spoke. "Truce, Hannah." He held out his hand.

Hannah took it without hesitation. Her grip was firm. "Truce."

He smiled. "This is not a promise to behave."

"I would have been disappointed if it were. I'm beginning to enjoy our battles."

"You're going to enjoy our loving even more."

"You never give up, do you?"

"Never. Not until I get what I want."

"And what is it you want, Jim Roman?"

"You."

He was whistling when he left the library. The massive carved door creaked shut behind him. Hannah looked around the peaceful book-lined room and wondered why, all of a sudden, it seemed so empty—and so dull.

"I won't waste a minute thinking about the West Coast Warrior," she said aloud, as if the sound of her own voice made her words more convincing, as if she could cleanse him from her mind by merely saying so.

Her feet tapped smartly against the wooden floor as she hurried from the room. There were a dozen wedding chores that needed her attention, but Jim Roman loomed large in her mind, overshadowing them all.

Jim had no idea where he was going when he left the room. All he knew was that he had to get away from Hannah. He was accustomed to being the aggressor. He needed to regroup before carrying out his plans for the delectable Dr. Donovan.

He detoured by the kitchen long enough to thank Anna for her invitation to the family supper and to decline politely. He was sidetracked by Tanner, who had just arrived from Dallas and wanted to show him the stables. Then he got into his rental car and headed into the city.

There was always something exciting to do in a city. He'd seen nothing of Greenville except the airport and the rural areas outside the city limits. He'd prowl the riverfront, locate an out-of-the-way dive. The best food and the best music were often found in unexpected places. Two things John had told him about the Mississippi Delta: The food was delicious, and the jazz was exquisite. He'd find out for himself.

Hannah told herself she wasn't listening for Jim's car. She rolled over and punched her pillow, then she lifted her head and peered at the clock. Three A.M. Where in the world was he? She hadn't seen him since he left her in the library. Of course, she thought, that didn't mean much. She'd been so busy with wedding preparations, she'd barely seen Tanner and Paul and their families after they'd arrived.

She thought she heard the scrunch of gravel under tires and cocked her head, listening, but it turned out to be a mouse in the wall.

"Hell's bells." She rose from the bed, secured her hair on top of her head with a couple of large combs, reached for her robe, and headed to the bathroom. On her way, she picked up a thick book, a horror story by Robert R. McCammon. If *Swan Song* couldn't take her mind off Jim Roman, nothing could.

She leaned over the tub and turned the water on full force. Then she searched the cabinets until she found what she wanted—the bubble bath. She poured in twice as much as she needed.

One of the luxuries she missed in Glacier Bay was a bubble bath. The cabin she lived in was strictly functional in design. It had one large room with a tiny cooking alcove, a sleeping loft, and a small bath. She was lucky to have a shower indoors: many of the cabins didn't.

She loved her work. For her it was the fulfillment of lifelong dream. The love of nature and all living things that had been fostered in her while growing up on the Donovan farm had come to full fruition when she'd received her Ph.D. and set out to study one of the world's most magnificent mammals, the whale. Her work was hard and demanding, usually carried out in remote places that precluded an ordinary life-style. And it was totally satisfying.

She wouldn't trade her primitive spot in Glacier Bay for all the luxuries in the world, but when she came home, she did enjoy her bubble baths. She was taking her second one of the day.

She sighed as she stepped into the water. Closing her eyes, she leaned back and let herself slide downward until she was up to the neck in glistening iridescent bubbles.

"I see you've already drawn my bath."

Hannah's eyes flew open.

Jim was leaning against the door frame, taking in the view. His hair was disheveled, his shirt was unbuttoned to the waist, and he had the satisfied look of a great leopard that has cornered its quarry. She felt a rush of adrenaline, a sure sign that her body was preparing itself for battle. Her gaze swung to his chest, which was smooth and hard and tanned. The rush she felt this time was heat. She shut her mind to what her body might be preparing itself to do.

"What are you doing in here?"

"I'm going to take a bath."

"The tub is occupied."

He grinned. "That's fine with me. I always like company in my bath."

"Well, I don't."

"Your actions contradict your words." His eyes never left hers as he peeled off his shirt and let it dangle carelessly from his left hand. Under the water, Hannah's hands tightened on the bar of soap. Unconsciously her tongue flicked over her lips. Jim advanced a step, tossing his shirt onto the vanity. "The door on my side of the bathroom was open, Hannah. I consider that an invitation." His hand went to his belt buckle.

"Don't you dare take off your pants."

"I dare many things, Hannah." He was looming over the tub now, so close she could see the precise way his chest hair disappeared into the top of his pants. She found herself staring, imagining the sexy-crisp touch of that chest hair against her breasts.

"Do you like what you see, my beautiful sleek wildcat?"

Lying would be useless. She knew he could see the truth in her eyes. "Yes." She gazed boldly at him. "I like what I see."

As they assessed each other, a handful of crystal bubbles disintegrated in the middle of the tub. One of Hannah's legs came into view. Seeing the gleam of lust in Jim's eyes, she brazenly lifted her leg high out of the tub and soaped it, taking her time, watching his face for signs that she was disturbing him. "I like what I see very much, Jim Roman—but I don't want it."

He chuckled. It was a low, satisfied growl of amusement that reverberated off the bathroom tiles. "I'll make you want it."

She slowly lowered her leg back into the water. Laughter wasn't what she'd wanted from him. She'd wanted him to retreat under her bold attack. "Men of your type don't appeal to me."

He put his right foot on the rim of the tub, propped his elbow on his bended knee, and leaned closer to her. He was still smiling.

"Is that why your face is flushed and your eyes are bedroom languid? Because I don't appeal to you?"

She felt as if she were smothering. She wanted nothing more than to take a big gulp of air, but she wouldn't give him the satisfaction of knowing how much he bothered her. "You've assessed me wrong. It's the heat."

His left hand reached out and lightly cupped her face. "Yes. It's the heat." There was a vibrant urgency in his voice that made her shiver. "Body heat. Yours and mine."

She closed her eyes for a moment, willing herself to be strong, steeling herself to resist temptation. She snapped them open and looked at him. "Remove your hand."

Laughing, he pulled back. "What's the matter, Hannah? Don't you like to play?"

"I like to choose my playmates."

"So do I. And I've already chosen you."

His eyes gleaming, he bent down and trailed his hands through the water. She held her breath as his fingers stopped only inches from her breast.

She could imagine his hand closing around her, massaging in the rough-tender way she liked. She wanted it, she ached for it, but she knew she couldn't have it. Jim Roman was a roaring blaze that would consume her. "If you touch me again, I'll black both your eyes."

His hand moved a fraction of an inch closer. "When I touch you, it will be because you want it. You'll ask me for it."

Their eyes locked in a battle of wills. Rage and excitement boiled through her. There was something else too. Something so powerful, so basic and primitive, she recognized it immediately. It was lust, her old enemy.

Her chin went up. "I wouldn't ask you to touch me if you were the last man on earth."

He merely smiled and lifted a brow. Then, leaning closer, he blew away the bubbles that covered her breasts. Her nipples suddenly jutted out of the water, tight and hard and ready.

His eyes gleaming, he whispered, "You'll ask me, Hannah." Abruptly he stood up. "Sleep well."

He was gone as quickly as he had come.

Hannah went limp. Leaning her head back against the cold porcelain, she put her hand over her racing heart.

With the scientific mind that was accustomed to analysis, Dr. Hannah Donovan came to a startling conclusion. She'd wanted Jim Roman to take her. At the precise moment he'd blown the bubbles away and looked at her with raw passion in his eyes, she'd wanted him as she'd never wanted another man.

She reached for her book and jerked it open. But the words were a jumble. Throwing her book onto the cabinet, she turned the hot water faucet on full force. Her water had gotten cold. Her bubbles were deflating too. Dripping water all over the floor and not caring, she got out of the tub, opened the cabinet, and took out the bubble bath. She dumped half the bottle in and climbed back in. Then, repenting over the puddle she'd left on the floor, she got out again and wiped it up with a dry towel.

When she straightened back up, she noticed Jim's shirt wadded onto the corner of the vanity. Against her better judgment she reached for it, clasped it in her hands, and brought it to her face. His scent clung there, the strong, masculine smells of sweat and spice and desire. She inhaled deeply. Her own passion flared. She felt moist and hot and as tightly strung as a cello waiting to be played. She knew that she was close to letting her emotions get out of hand.

"Hell's bells."

She tossed the shirt away, got back into the tub, leaned her head on the cool porcelain, and shut her eyes. For the first time in her life she was going to ignore a problem instead of trying to solve it.

Jim leaned against the bathroom door. The sounds of Hannah's fury filtered through. She was a quarry worthy of the hunt, he decided.

Leaving the door, he stripped and walked to the window. There was nothing outside except a wide sweep of lawn guarded by one giant magnolia and a line of mighty oaks. There was no neon, no concrete, no billboards, no skyscrapers. The silence made his skin crawl. He pressed his face to the glass, but the only sound he heard was the faint chirping of crickets.

He walked to his bed, an old-fashioned cherry four-poster, and lay down. He sank so far into the soft mattress, he thought it would take a forklift to pull him out. The sheet he pulled over his chest smelled like April flowers in the rain. All the comforts of home. And yet, it wasn't home to him.

He was bone tired—from the long trip, the change in hours, and his evening of mild debauchery—but he couldn't sleep. He lay still, unconsciously listening for jets flying overhead, the far-off sound of freeway traffic, the drunken squabbling of the wharf bums, and the lapping of the Pacific Ocean against his houseboat.

Three

Jim awoke to the smell of coffee and the sound of laughter.

Instantly alert, he walked to the window and looked down. The blonde caught his eye first. She possessed the beautiful serenity of an angel. She was laughing at something the tall dark-haired man beside her was saying. As he watched, the man bent down and caught the angelic woman in an embrace. Suddenly three sturdy hellions catapulted themselves at the couple, tugging at their hands and the woman's skirt, laughing and squealing. The man lifted the smallest child, a dark-haired boy of about four, onto his shoulder, and the woman took the other two by the hands. All five of them raced toward the rope swing hanging from the fat limb of an oak tree.

A family, Jim thought. Probably the minister, Paul Donovan, and his wife and children. The description fit. He remembered the way Anna's face had glowed when she'd talked about her children and grandchildren.

Jim turned from the window and reached for his pants. As he pulled them on, he thought of his own family, his mother, her hands gnarled from hard work and her face lined from worry, and his father—Brick Roman. A big, handsome sailor whose love for the sea finally outweighed whatever affection he'd had for his wife and son. When Jim had been eight, Brick had sailed off on the *The Black Rover* and had never come back. Over the years they got a few cards postmarked from exotic, faraway places such as Tahiti and Fiji and New Guinea and Indonesia. Some years they even got Christmas presents—coconut shells with carved faces, pink seashells strung together in a necklace, a bamboo wind chime—usually wrapped in wrinkled Santa Claus paper and arriving two months after Christmas had passed.

His mother displayed the useless gifts on their sagging mantel and went about the business of scrubbing other people's floors, while he sewed another patch on his pants and went into the streets to see if he could hustle up a few dimes by being somebody's errand boy.

All that had changed now, of course. The gifts and cards had stopped coming many years before, and Mary Roman lived in a neat white frame house in a neighborhood with parks and playgrounds and schools and law-abiding citizens. He provided for her. Just as he would someday provide for a wife.

That was his dream—to find a sweet, old-fashioned girl, someone he could take care of, someone he could provide for. He'd give up his houseboat and build a small white cottage with a picket fence and rambling roses, somewhere near the water, close enough to smell the sea but within hearing distance of a brash, brawling, neon-and-concrete city.

He smiled at his own simple fantasy. The American dream. He'd have it someday. He'd have the same sort of healthy, happy, well-loved, cared-for family he'd glimpsed out the window. Someday. But not yet.

For now he'd content himself with covering the Donovan wedding and taming the Donovan wildcat.

He had one arm in his shirt-sleeve when he heard the laughter, deep and throaty and sexy. Hannah's laughter, he thought. It had to be. No other woman had a voice quite like hers, a husky musical voice that made him think of a slow, sexy blues song.

He hurried to the window. Hannah was there, leaning down from a white stallion, laughing at something her brother was saying. Jim's shirt dangled in his hand, forgotten. The beauty of woman and horse twisted his gut. Hannah leaned low in the saddle, her hair a bolt of black silk against the pristine white of the horse's neck. Her expression was soft and gentle and loving.

Jim had a sudden vision of Hannah in his bed, her midnight hair piled against the pillows, her soft expression aimed exclusively at him. His breath became short; his loins tightened.

"Fool," he chided himself. "She's not the fireside, homemaking type." He turned from the window, vowing to think of her only as a conquest, something to help pass his time in Greenville. But that vision of her, leaning low in the saddle, woman-soft and laughing, wouldn't go away.

As he headed down the stairs, he knew what he

was going to do, what he *had* to do. He was going riding.

Hannah was in the pasture behind the barn, just as he'd hoped. He stood beside the barn for a moment, drinking in the sight of her. She rode hard and fast, thundering over the ground on the white stallion. Her exultant, throaty laughter carried to him on the morning breeze. Animal and woman seemed to be one, their bodies flowing with the movement of the horse's hooves. There was a grace in the horse and rider that complemented the morning.

Jim lingered a moment longer, silently appreciating the scene, then he went inside the barn and led out a chestnut filly. He arranged the saddle blanket and was hefting the saddle upward when he heard the stallion whinny. It was a high-pitched sound of alarm that sent shivers up his spine.

He whirled around and saw them across the pasture fence—Hannah's white stallion rearing on its hind legs, its forelegs beating the air, and Hannah, bent low over its neck, fighting to keep her seat.

Jim dropped the saddle and vaulted onto the filly's back. Praying that Tanner had been right about the chestnut's jumping abilities, Jim urged the filly on, racing toward the fence and calculating the exact moment when he would jump.

A burst of adrenaline pumped through him; his senses became knife-edge sharp. In the distance he could see Hannah's spooked horse, rearing and plunging back down.

"Hold him, Hannah." Jim scarely was aware that

he'd cried out to her. His own horse rose in the air. For a breathless moment it seemed to be suspended over the fence. Time stood still for Jim. He was committed. There was no pulling back. His horse would either clear the fence or come crashing down, possibly killing them both.

Suddenly he felt the ground under him. The chestnut filly had landed smoothly and was racing across the pasture without a break in its stride. Exultant, Jim yelled once more, "Hold him, little wildcat."

Hannah's stallion bolted. At least her seat was sure now, Jim thought as he galloped after her. He leaned over his filly's neck, urging her forward in Apache language he'd learned from his friend Colter Gray Wolf.

The filly was smaller than the stallion, but she used her size to her advantage. She flew across the pasture, rapidly closing the distance between herself and the stallion. Big chunks of earth flew up from the pounding hooves; dust swirled around them.

Jim planned his move, judged his distance, and closed in. When the horses were side by side, he reached out and lifted Hannah from the saddle. With his arm firmly around her small waist, he held her, suspended, for a small eternity while he maneuvered the chestnut away from the stallion. Then, with split-second timing, he swung her up behind him. Her arms instantly circled his waist, and he could feel her heart thudding against his back.

He reined the filly to a stop beside a small creek. Hannah still clung to him. He closed his hands over hers. They felt soft and small and exceedingly vulnerable.

"Hannah," he said, turning slightly so he could see her over his shoulder. "Are you all right?"

"Yes." He loved the breathless quality of her voice and the flush on her face. She didn't look like a woman who had just been rescued from a runaway horse; she looked like a woman who'd been thoroughly loved. "Yes," she said again. Her voice was stronger this time, and she smiled. "It was magnificent."

"Magnificent?"

"Absolutely magnificent. Where did you learn to ride like that?"

Jim chuckled. "You're quite a woman. Do you know that, Hannah Donovan? Any other woman in your position would be shaking and probably crying—and you're asking where I learned to ride."

"Well? Are you going to tell me?"

Instead of answering, he swung off the horse, then he reached up and helped her down. Even when her feet touched the ground, his hands lingered on her waist. Gazing at her, he forgot all about her question. He couldn't remember the last time he'd held such a tempting bundle in his arms. She was soft and flushed and laughing, very much a woman. Looking into her bright face, he thought how easy it would be to take her. Right there. On the grass. Her guard was down; she was feeling grateful. He almost lowered her to the ground, but an untimely attack of honor held him back.

Instead, his hands tightened on her waist. Stepping in so close their thighs touched, he studied her. He saw the tip of her pink tongue flick out and slowly circle her lips. A small trickle of sweat rolled down the side of her face.

"You're hot."

"Yes. It's the excitement of the ride."

His eyes searched her face, then swung downward to the tiny pulse spot at the base of her throat. It was fluttering like a captive hummingbird. "No. It's us, Hannah."

She grew very still. "I won't let it be."

"Why?"

Instead of answering, she changed the subject with a question of her own. "Who taught you to ride?"

"My friend. Colter Gray Wolf."

"Indian?"

"Apache."

"Awww." The way she said it, in a long-drawn-out sigh, made him think of love sounds. His right hand slid downward, slowly tracing the curve of her hips, and slipped over her blue-jean-clad thigh until it was resting on the fullest part of her buttocks. With a subtle shifting he brought her hips into his. They were a perfect fit.

She made the small sound again. "Awww." He didn't know if it was a sound of wonder or satisfaction or need. All he knew was that it wrapped around him like velvet. His passion blossomed.

Her eyes widened, the blue deeper than ever. "An exotic man," she whispered. "I once knew an exotic man. How did you meet Colter Gray Wolf?"

Jim didn't want to talk abut Colter Gray Wolf; he wanted to ask about her exotic man. Who in the hell was he, and why did her voice go soft and dreamy when she spoke of him? The vehemence of his feelings surprised him. That was no way to tame the Donovan hellcat, he told himself. He firmly squashed his maverick jealousy and answered her question.

"Several years ago he dragged me out of a waterfront bar and patched me up. He's a doctor."

She reached up and touched the faint scar on his forehead. "This?" Her hand gently followed the scar line across his forehead to his eyebrow.

"Yes." He covered her hand with his, pressing it against his face.

"I'm glad."

Jim smiled. "Glad he patched me up or glad he taught me to ride?"

"Both." Her tongue flicked over her lips again. He leaned forward, imagining the feel of that tongue on his flesh. "I would have been all right, you know."

"Would you?"

"Yes. I ride well."

She made a small move to free her hand. Reluctantly he let it go.

"I've known that from the beginning."

His free hand circled the back of her neck. She didn't try to pull out of his embrace. Ever so slowly, he inched his hand upward, lifting her hair. He closed his eyes for a moment, enjoying the sensations of soft, downy skin and soft, silky hair. Of all the places on a woman's body, the back of the neck was one of his favorites, probably because it was such a vulnerable spot. If he'd cared to delve into the psychology of it, he'd most likely come up with something regarding his need to control. But psychology was as far from his mind as San Francisco. Right now he had the moment, and he had a curiously gentle Hannah in his arms.

He opened his eyes and watched her luxuriant black hair sift through his fingers. "From the moment I saw you, I've known," he whispered.

"We're not talking about horses now, are we?" she said softly.

"No."

"I probably would have been better off with the snake."

He kept his hand on the back of her neck, gently massaging.

"Is that what spooked your horse?"

"Yes. A cottonmouth moccasin, I think. Sometimes they crawl up from the creek."

"I should be feeling very grateful to that snake."

"Why?"

"You're here . . . in my arms." His hips shifted subtly against hers. "Where I want you to be."

"I'm in your arms because I choose to be."

He didn't say anything; he merely quirked an eyebrow in question.

"I barely slept last night for thinking of you," she continued. "One of the reasons I went riding this morning was to wipe you from my mind."

He smiled. "Did it work?"

"No. You were very much with me. Then, when my horse spooked and you pulled that Apache rescue stunt, I was suddenly face-to-face with the man who had haunted my dreams."

Her honesty delighted him. And for some strange reason, his very delight in her made him wary. The spunky, spicy, sexy woman he'd chased so relentlessly was finally in his arms, confessing that she was there willingly, and he felt an unusual reluctance to do anything about it.

"I like you this way, Hannah—soft and feminine and vulnerable."

"I'm a woman, Jim . . ."

"A fact that never fails to escape my notice."

"A woman who knows exactly what she is doing."

Smiling, he lifted a hand and cupped her flushed cheek. "And what are you doing, my beautiful wildcat?"

"I'm testing myself."

"You call this a test?" He hauled her so hard against his chest, her breath whooshed out. "I call it an invitation."

"You call everything an invitation." Slowly she put her arms around his neck. "I'm testing my control." Pulling his head down, she traced his lips with her tongue. He waited, simmering from the heat of her nearness and from the heat of the morning sun. "You see, Jim, I once lost control with a man, and I intend to see that it never happens again. I'm in your arms to prove to myself that I can walk away— untouched."

"You may walk away, Hannah, but it won't be untouched."

He took her mouth fiercely, savagely. His tongue slipped between her parted lips and plundered without mercy. The passion he'd sensed in her erupted. Small love sounds escaped her lips, and she pressed herself so close, their bodies seemed to be one.

Jim exulted in the feel of her—her firm slender body; her hair, whisper-soft and silky; her lips, lush and hot. Special. The word sang through his mind. This woman was special.

Unconsciously he gentled the kiss, slanting his lips tenderly across hers. The heady sweetness drugged him.

"Hannah." He sighed against her lips. "My Hannah."

"No." She pulled back a fraction of an inch, her

breathing heavy. "I can't be yours . . . heaven help me . . . one last taste." Her lips were on his again.

She savored him for one final heart-stopping moment before pulling away. Then she drew the tattered edges of her control around her like a protective cape. Raking her hand through her disheveled hair, she looked him squarely in the eye. "That was a nice try, Jim, but I'm not touched."

He roared with mirth. "You lie so beautifully. If it wasn't for that bedroom look in your eyes, I'd almost believe you." He turned away nonchalantly and reached for the reins of his horse.

"What are you doing?"

"I thought I'd catch that white stallion so you'd have a ride back to the barn"—he vaulted onto the filly and grinned down at her—"unless you have another mount in mind."

Hannah suppressed her grin. Jim's wickedness reminded her of her own irrepressible brothers, especially Tanner and Jacob. Besides that, his devil-may-care attitude helped dilute the spell of passion she was under.

"If that's an offer to ride with you, I'll stay here with the snakes."

"You're more than a match for them, Hannah."

"Why, thank you. You say the most romantic things."

"I try."

"By the way, I expect that's all you'll be doing with El Diablo—trying. Tanner and I are the only ones who can handle him."

Jim chuckled. "Yesterday when Tanner showed me his horses, I had the stallion eating out of my hand. I'll be back before you can miss me, Hannah."

She shaded her eyes against the sun and watched Jim ride toward the stallion. Just as she had predicted, El Diablo bolted at Jim's approach. She wasn't sure what happened next. All she knew was that she'd witnessed another example of Jim's remarkable horsemanship. The sound of pounding horse's hooves echoed around the pasture as the small chestnut filly closed on the stallion. Suddenly Jim was in the air, flying across the space between the horses. Then he was in El Diablo's saddle.

The stallion, recognizing a master's touch, trotted obediently back to the creek, proudly bearing his new rider and leading the filly.

Jim slid from the saddle, lifted Hannah off her feet, and set her unceremoniously on the filly. "The stallion is too much horse for you to handle, wildcat."

Before Hannah could protest, he was trotting off, leading her bridle as if she were a child. No man ever had dared treat her in such a high-handed manner. But then, no other man was called the West Coast Warrior. It was more than a name, she thought: It was a description. Jim Roman was a warrior in every sense of the word.

"Are you taking me captive?"

"The thought did occur to me." He moved the big stallion in close enough to pat Hannah's cheek. "But I prefer that you come to me, wildcat."

She fought the quick rush of desire that surged through her. "Never."

He didn't say a word, but his actions spoke volumes. He quirked an eyebrow upward in that sardonic, wicked way of his and grinned.

Hannah knew she had been bested. Instead of

feeling anger, she felt a strange kind of triumph. On the heels of the triumph came the old wariness.

Turning her head away from the West Coast Warrior, she rode the rest of the way to the barn in silence, plotting her revenge for his tyranny.

Hannah was saved further battling with Jim by the arrival of a lavender Eldorado Cadillac convertible. As the horses rounded the barn, the convertible came to a gravel-scattering stop in the front yard. The driver pressed the horn, and a raucus metallic rendition of "Alabama Jubilee" split the air.

"Hallie's home."

Jim watched as a carbon copy of Hannah emerged from the car. Wearing a Stetson and cowboy boots and surrounded by two Great Danes and a huge, smiling man, Hallie didn't merely step from the car: She made a grand entrance into the yard, like a brass band. No wonder Josh Butler was smiling, Jim thought. He was a hell of a lucky guy to have a woman like Hallie.

His gaze swung around to Hannah, who sat atop the chestnut filly with the air of a a sleek, exotic cat waiting its chance to pounce. Lord help the man who hitched his fate to Hannah's.

The Donovans poured from the house to greet Hallie and her fiancé.

Everybody started talking at once. Somehow a little order finally crept into the chaos. Breakfast was served, bags were carried upstairs, and various groups were formed.

After he had insisted on cleaning up the kitchen—and won—Jim went off to interview Hallie and Josh while Hannah accompanied her mother and her brother Paul to the church.

Hannah knew she should be feeling relieved that she no longer had to battle with the indomitable Jim Roman. Instead, she felt deprived.

She loitered on the church steps, thinking of all the ways Jim outraged her and of all the ways he made her blood sing. Heaven help the woman who walked down the aisle with the West Coast Warrior.

She was grinning when she went inside the church to help with her sister's wedding preparations.

Four

"You're breathtaking, Hallie."

Hannah sat on an old steamer trunk in the attic, watching as her sister modeled the gown she would wear for her wedding.

It had been a hectic day. After she and her mother and Paul had left the church, they'd gone by the florist shop, then stopped for a consultation with the organist. This was the first breather she'd had.

"You think so?" Hallie lifted the antique lace veil from a box in an ancient armoire and arranged it on her head. "I don't smell like mothballs, do I?"

Hannah laughed. "How could you smell like mothballs? Mom's been getting that dress ready since the day you called and said you were going to be married. She keeps it up here in Granny's armoire only for sentimental reasons."

"I thought the day would never come." Hallie gazed off into the distance. "Do you think Jacob will make it?"

"I'm certain of it. He'd never miss anything as important as your wedding."

"You're right. He'll come in from some faraway place, laughing at all of us for being worried." Hallie backed up to her sister. "Undo me, please."

Hannah began unfastening the tiny pearl buttons on their grandmother's wedding dress. "It all worked out for you, didn't it? Just the way I told you it would."

"Better than I ever imagined. Josh's brother seems to be fully recovered from his alcoholism, and his dad—" Hallie paused, laughing. "Hiram has become quite a live wire. He's a favorite around the theater with my special children. And the best news of all is that he's getting married."

"To that fiesty woman you told me about, your landlady?"

"Yes. Her name is Debbie. They'll be here tonight for the rehearsal dinner." Hallie carefully slipped the dress over her head and began to arrange it on its padded hanger. Suddenly she turned to her sister and held out the dress. "You try it, Hannah."

"Who? Me? I won't be wearing a wedding dress."

"That's what I thought, too, until a very special sister told me I couldn't keep ignoring my feelings." Hallie hung up the wedding dress, then sat down beside Hannah and wrapped her arm around her sister. "Rai Ghayami happened a long time ago. I don't like to see you denying yourself so much pleasure because of one unhappy affair."

"You know me too well."

"Shouldn't I?" Hallie pointed to their reflections in the mirror. "You're like an extension of myself; I feel what you feel. Sometimes I'm even sick when you're sick. Remember the chicken pox?"

Hannah laughed. "How could I forget? You were at Camp Tik-a-witha, and I was on the Gulf Coast with Uncle Matt and Aunt Lettie. We broke out with chicken pox on the same day."

"It's eerie sometimes."

"Yes, it is." Hannah eyed the wedding dress. "Thank goodness love isn't catching."

"If it were a contagious disease, I'd try to give it to you."

"Why?"

"Because I know that you have a great capacity to love."

"I love my work and my whales and my dogs. . . ."

"It's not enough. I love my work, too, but I'd be bereft without Josh."

"I'm not bereft, Hallie."

"I know that, but you're missing so much joy by not giving love a chance."

"I gave it a chance once."

"You made one mistake, just as I did."

Hannah stood up and smoothed an imaginary wrinkle in the wedding gown. "Just listen to you, going on like Ann Landers and Dr. Ruth. Is that the way I sound when I give advice?"

Hallie laughed. "Precisely. How does it feel when the shoe is on the other foot?"

"I can't say that I like being told what I should do. I'd much rather do the telling."

"From now on you can. This is my first and last lecture."

"What brought it on?"

"I don't know. I guess I want everybody to be as

happy as I am." Lifting the skirt of the wedding dress, Hallie held it against her chest. "You don't think it's tacky, wearing a white satin gown the second time around?"

"Since when has a Donovan ever worried about appearances? Take my advice, Hallie. Wear it."

Hallie kissed her on the cheek. "Take mine, too, Hannah."

Hannah chuckled. "Not a chance. That domestic scene is not for me."

"Someday somebody will come along to make you change your mind. And when he does, I hope he's at least half as wonderful as Josh."

With a gay wave and a lilting laugh, Hallie skipped down the attic stairs.

Hannah sat down on the trunk and stared at the wedding dress. She was still for so long, she was certain spiders had built their webs around her. The tiny beam of sunshine slanting through the attic window moved westward until it was shining directly across the white satin dress. The golden glow gave the wedding dress a mystic quality.

Slowly Hannah rose and walked toward the dress. Her hands caressed the satin folds of the skirt, then moved upward to the lace and pearls of the bodice. Almost against her will she took the dress from the hanger.

Hallie had told Jim where to find Hannah.

In the manner of the Apache, he silently climbed the attic stairs and pushed open the door. What he saw took his breath away. Hannah was dressed in a wedding gown. A beam of sunlight from the high attic window played over the white satin dress, danced over her creamy skin and her sable hair. She shimmered. She'd was an exotic, gorgeous woman, but in the wedding dress she was achingly beautiful.

Jim leaned in the doorway, watching. He knew he was seeing an illusion. Hannah was a wildcat through and through. She was not this soft, lovely creature who made him think of lace curtains at the window and slippers by the fire. In spite of all reason, he drank in the sight of her, imagined her with the wind in her hair, standing on the deck of his house-boat, waiting for him to come home.

He didn't know how long he would have stood there if she hadn't turned. Her indigo eyes widened.

Jim ducked his head under the low doorway and stalked Hannah. He didn't stop until he was close enough to touch her. Some trick of fate had turned her into his dream girl; he had to see for himself that she was the same bold woman he wanted to catch but not to keep.

She caught her breath as he reached up and adjusted her wedding veil. "I didn't know the bride had eyes as blue as the Mediterranean."

"I'm not the bride."

"Then why are you dressed in white? Practicing?"

"Certainly not. I never intend to marry."

"You know what they say about the best intentions."

"Not in this case." She reached up to take the veil off her head, but Jim's hands stopped her.

"Don't." His eyes burned across her face. "I want to look at you a moment longer."

Hannah held her breath. She was caught, and there was nothing to do but make the best of it. As Jim's dark eyes raked over her, she cursed the fates that he had been the one to catch her parading around in her grandmother's wedding dress.

"Why are you here, Jim?"

His hands left the wedding veil and bracketed her cheeks. "I felt the need for some excitement, Hannah."

"You've come to the wrong place."

"I think not. You're the most exciting woman I know."

His hands felt gentle on her face. She wished he wouldn't touch her like that. She already was feeling sentimental, and his sweet touch was sending her right over the edge.

"Please," she whispered.

"Please what, Hannah?" Even his voice was gentle. She felt as if she were falling into a tender trap.

"Please take your hands away from my face."

Instead of obeying, he tipped her face up toward his. "Do I bother you, little wildcat?"

"More than you'll ever know."

Her remark seemed to please him. His smile was that of a man who knew he'd devastated a woman. That's what he was doing, she decided—devastating her. Whether it was their proximity or too many years of denial or merely his own overpowering presence, she didn't know; furthermore, she didn't want to know. She simple wanted to survive Jim Roman's invasion of her quiet Delta home and get back to the work she loved.

"More than your exotic man?" he asked suddenly.

She jerked out of his reach. "What?"

Jim crammed his hands into his pockets and began to pace the small, cramped attic. "You mentioned an exotic man this morning. Who is he?"

"That's none of your business."

"Anything that keeps a gorgeous woman from my bed is my business."

"Why, you arrogant jackass." She jerked the pins from the wedding veil and pulled it from her hair. Turning her back on Jim, she folded the veil into the box. "I wouldn't come to your bed if you were begging me on bended knee."

"Is that why you kiss me the way you do?"

"I kiss all men that way."

He was behind her, turning her in his arms. "Even your exotic man?" His eyes blazed down into hers. "Who is he?"

The heat of his touch coursed through her. Her passion threatened to consume her. She willed herself back under control.

Keeping her voice level, she glared at him. "His name is Rai Ghayami, and he was more man than you will ever be."

She saw the power in Jim's gaze mere seconds before his mouth crushed down on hers. She had meant to hold herself stiff against him this time, but there was a savage fury in the kiss that shook her resolve. Something in her rose to meet that power.

One of them groaned—she wasn't sure who—then they were clinging to each other, their bodies rocking together in the love battle they knew so well. She felt his hands working the small buttons on the back of her dress, felt the satin and lace being slipped from her shoulders. His lips left hers and burned across her throat, then moved downward to sear along the tops of her breasts.

She leaned her head back, unconsciously offering

herself up to him while still telling herself that she was in complete control.

Suddenly she felt herself being pushed away. Holding the wedding dress over her breasts, she looked at Jim. He had the bewildered look of a man who had set out to trap a wild animal and found himself the quarry.

"If he was so much man, he would never have let you go." With that gruff-voiced declaration, he turned and stalked away. He was moving so fast, she thought he would behead himself on the attic doorway, but at the last minute he ducked under.

Hannah finished the job Jim had started: She pulled the wedding dress off. What would have happened, she wondered, if he had been the one to take it off? Judging by the way she felt, she decided the answer was fairly simple. She'd have given in to her passion.

Hanging the wedding dress carefully in the old armoire, Hannah came to a decision. She wanted Jim Roman and so she would have him—in her own way and in her own time. She'd go to him to slake the burning thirst that raged through her. The West Coast Warrior's bed would be her proving ground. Once and for all she'd show herself that she could satisfy the needs of her body without sacrificing her career.

Her lips curved upward into a smile. Jim Roman had been right. She'd go to him. Once. Then she'd walk away.

Her smile broadened as she reached for her clothes. She'd go to him all right, but first she'd have her revenge.

• • •

Jim cursed himself all the way down the attic stairs.

He didn't know what had happened up there. He'd gone to Hannah, looking for some excitement, then he'd seen her in the white satin dress. It was the damned wedding dress that had made a fool of him, he decided. For a moment he'd believed Hannah was the soft, feminine woman he'd been searching for. He'd even gone so far as to be jealous of her exotic man. Good Lord, he thought. Jealous! What he needed was a good stiff drink.

He climbed into his rented car and drove to the little dive he'd discovered down on the waterfront. It was cool and dark inside, with nothing to mar the quiet except the tinkle of glasses on the polished bar and the unhurried rhythm of a lonesome blues song from the upright piano in the corner. Jim chose a table at the back of the bar near a window. Outside, the afternoon sun danced on the river.

Jim slouched into his chair, content. The sight of water always soothed him. He supposed he'd inherited that trait from his father. As the waiter brought his drink and the plaintive blues song washed over him, he wondered what other traits he'd inherited from Brick Roman. Not wanderlust. He was happy with his houseboat by the Pacific. What about irresponsibility? Was that why Brick had left, or was there some other reason? It was an old puzzle without an answer.

Reaching for his drink, Jim impatiently cast aside thoughts of his father. He turned his face to the window, seeking solace in the river. Instead of water, he saw a woman in white, a bold, exciting, irresistible woman who threatened to turn all his dreams upside down.

His glass clinked against Formica as he set it back on the table. Outside his window the setting sun put on a spectactular show. Around him, the blues wailed on. But Jim neither saw nor heard: He simply sat in his chair with his untouched glass of bourbon, seeing the image of Hannah in a white satin wedding gown.

The image of Hannah in the wedding dress stayed with Jim through the rehearsal that evening and followed him to the country club for the rehearsal dinner. Even though she was dressed in red, he still remembered the shimmering innocence of her in white.

He wondered if he might be losing his mind.

"You've hardly said a word all evening. Surely we're not that boring."

Wishes did come true, he thought as Hannah moved into the chair recently vacated by Aunt Agnes. All evening he'd watched her, willing her to come to him. And now she was at his side, as vivid and glowing as a scarlet poppy. She looked as if she'd just stepped off a roller coaster and had loved every minute of the ride. The image of her in pure white shattered with an almost audible tinkle.

"I've been busy taking mental notes," he lied.

"I forgot. You have a story to write." She laughed. "I hope you aren't going to tell the whole truth."

"No. I'm going to leave out the part about you outshining the bride."

"That's not possible. She's radiant."

"So are you."

She leaned toward him and gazed earnestly into his face. "You really mean that, don't you?"

"Yes. For tonight, I've put all my ulterior motives aside."

"Please don't be too nice, Jim."

"Why not? I thought it might give us both a little relief from the skirmish."

"It makes what I have to do harder."

Jim found it impossible not to touch her when she was near. He reached out and caught a dark, shiny strand of her hair. It wrapped around his fingers as intimately as a kiss.

"And what is that, my gorgeous red vamp?"

"I have to deliver your comeuppance to you."

He quirked his eyebrow upward. "For the horse?"

"You know darned well it's for the horse."

"If this is going to be as good as what you delivered in the tub, I can hardly wait."

She grinned. "I knew that goody twoshoes act wouldn't last."

"It's not my style, but I try sometimes."

"I like you better when you're being your usual arrogant, overbearing self."

"Then I'll strive not to disappoint you." He cupped the back of her neck and pulled her close for a quick, hard kiss.

Around them, the noise and laughter of the wedding party went on unheeded. The bride and groom slipped out the door to spend the rest of the evening alone, and some Donovans began to make their way home while others hung around to swap family tales. They paid Hannah and Jim no attention whatsoever.

Hannah pulled back from Jim, laughing. "If you thought you'd scandalize me, you've failed. I could pull off every stitch and parade stark naked down the middle of the dinner table, and nobody in my family would even bat an eyelash. Nobody loves a good prank better than a Donovan."

"You call that kiss a prank? I see I'll have to polish my technique. Perhaps you could help me."

"Perhaps."

Jim knew that wicked smile was coming, and when it did, he was shocked at how much he'd been counting on it

"Even better," he said, imitating her drawl, "why don't you do that little trick on the dinner table?"

"I have a better idea."

"I can't imagine anything more enticing than seeing you naked on the dinner table."

"How about a game of poker?"

"Strip?"

"Maybe. If you promise not to beat my pants off."

"That's the general idea."

Hannah stood up, taking his hand. "I have a room all set up."

Jim only had to look at her face to see that she was up to devilment.

"You've already planned this?"

"Of course."

"Revenge, I take it."

"Only if I win."

Jim grinned. "Then prepare to lose, Dr. Donovan. Poker is my game."

Hannah led him to a small back room of the country club. Three of her brothers—Tanner, Theo, and

Charles—already were there, sitting around a table, waiting for them. A deck of cards lay facedown on the snowy white tablecloth.

Tanner looked up and grinned. "What took you so long, Hannah?"

Theo winked at Charles. "Your lipstick's smeared, sis."

Hannah dragged out a chair and sat down, as unflustered as if she were on a Sunday school picnic. "Is nothing sacred around here?"

"Certainly not your love life." Tanner reached for the cards.

Hannah grinned at Jim. "All the Donovans are crazy. You can back out if you want to."

He pulled out the chair next to hers and deliberately pulled it so close that their thighs were touching when he sat down. "Getting cold feet, Hannah?"

"Not a chance," she shot back.

He turned to Tanner. "Name the game."

"Draw poker. Penny ante."

The bidding was quick and lively. Hannah beat them all the first game by bluffing with a pair of fours. From the cool, confident way she played, Jim had been certain that she was holding a full house.

Tanner laughed at the bewildered look on Jim's face. "She worked her way through graduate school playing poker."

"Don't believe a word he says. He's just jealous because I always beat him." Hannah picked up the cards. "My deal."

She took the second game too. And the third and the fourth. The stack of pennies in front of her grew.

"This is getting too rich for my blood," Charles

announced. "I'm already out twenty-five cents." He stood up to leave.

"Mine too." Theo joined him.

Tanner tossed the cards toward Hannah. "As much as I'd like to stay and get revenge, I have more exciting things to do."

Hannah grinned. "Give Amanda my love. And tell her thanks for letting me borrow you for a while."

The Donovan men took their boisterous leave, and Jim was left alone with Hannah. His gaze sizzled over her. The only sign that his scrutiny bothered her was the heightened color of her cheeks and the quick movement of her hands as she shuffled the cards.

At last he broke the silence. "I always thought I wanted a sweet old-fashioned girl."

"Don't you?"

"You make me wonder."

Hannah had meant to give some flip reply and get on with her revenge, but as she looked at Jim, she felt the slow, burning heat ignite deep inside her. With a start she realized it was more than passion, more than a passing attraction. She was responding to the person he was, the warm, witty, altogether *nice* man who fit into her family with grace and ease. She'd watched him charm her mother, win over her father and her brothers, and delight her nieces and nephews. She'd even watched him settle her mother into a chair with a cup of coffee while he cleaned up the breakfast dishes for the entire Donovan clan.

The cards fluttered to the table, silent. "You make me wonder too," she said.

"Wonder what?"

"Wonder if I've made the right choices. Wonder if my work will always be enough."

"Do you want to call the whole thing off, Hannah?"

She was still for a while, thinking over his proposition.

"How much of it?"

"The revenge."

"Merely the revenge?"

He laughed. "Only the revenge. The challenge was mine. It stands."

Ahhh, she thought, *he's a dangerous man.* Hannah had always loved danger. She supposed that was one of the reasons she kept exploring the depths of the ocean: There was always the danger—and the mystery.

"Nothing is called off." Smiling, she picked up the cards and began to shuffle. "Strip poker, Jim. Ante up."

He grinned. "My coat against your dress."

"Done."

Five

Hannah still had her dress.

Jim had lost his coat on the first round. He'd been holding a pair of queens, but Hannah had bluffed him out of the coat with a pair of fives. Sitting in his shirt-sleeves, he watched the expert way Hannah shuffled the cards.

"I admire your style, Dr. Donovan. Beginner's luck becomes you."

She gave him a madonna smile and kept on shuffling.

"If that smile is meant to take my mind off the game, it didn't work. I intend to see you naked."

"What will it be this time, Jim," she asked smoothly as she laid the cards on the table for him to cut, "your shirt or your pants?"

"My shirt against your shoes."

"Only my shoes?"

"I like to undress a woman bit by bit—saving the best till last."

Luck was with Hannah. Although she'd bluffed to

win the first hand, she was holding a sure thing the second time around—three of a kind. She tried to keep a poker face as Jim unbuttoned his shirt. He made a great show of it, pinning her to the chair with a sizzling gaze, taking his own sweet time with each button, acting as if he were stripping for an audience of thousands instead of losing his shirt at poker. The whole performance made her feel hot and irritated. She fanned herself with the cards.

Jim chuckled. "You could turn your head, you know."

"What?"

"If the sight of my chest bothers you that much, you could look the other way."

She flung the cards onto the table. "The sight of your chest doesn't bother me at all. I've seen marvelous chests before. I have brothers, you know."

He decided to be charitable and not point out her obvious slip of the tongue. As he handed her his shirt, he decided that losing this game was even better than winning. It pleased him to see the cool Dr. Hannah Donovan in such a flustered state.

"What do you want of mine this time, Doctor? My pants?"

She struggled to regain her composure. "What I want is for you to show a little more anxiety over losing."

"Shall I beat my chest? Or better yet"—he leaned across the table and said softly—"*you* pound my chest."

"Your deal," she said curtly.

She took his pants with a pair of twos. She'd played with such brazen abandon that he'd thought she had been holding at least a straight. Or perhaps he hadn't been thinking at all, he decided, as he rose to take off his pants. Maybe he'd fallen under the spell of her bewitching grin.

His gaze never left hers as he reached for his belt buckle.

"Do you want to call it quits while you're ahead, Dr. Donovan?"

There was a slight hesitation before she spoke. "Absolutely not."

"You're sure?"

She tossed her hair in a gesture of defiant bravado. "What's the matter, West Coast Warrior? Afraid of what I'll do to you?"

"No, wildcat. I'm afraid of what I'll do to you." His zipper was loud in the pulsing silence of the room.

Hannah squeezed her hands together in her lap. She'd be damned if she'd give Jim the satisfaction of knowing they were shaking.

His pants hit the floor with a magnified boom. She sat ramrod straight as he bent over, picked them up, and handed them to her.

"Your winnings."

She took a deep, steadying breath before she accepted the pants. Why he ever covered up that body with clothes was a mystery to her. She lost the next two hands, primarily, she decided, because she couldn't keep her eyes off him.

Minus shoes and earrings, she looked down at her hand. "I bet everything," she said as cool as iced lemonade.

"Everything, Hannah?" He quirked one eyebrow in question. He was holding a full house. "You can't escape under the cover of bubbles this time."

Her gaze swept over his bare chest, and she smiled. "Everything."

"What if you lose, Hannah? I'll take all of it, you know, every scrap of clothes you're wearing."

"So will I."

"In that case, I call."

There was a breathless moment while they merely looked into each other's eyes. He thought she was the boldest, most flamboyant, most exciting woman he'd ever met. A pity he wanted an old-fashioned girl.

She thought he was the brashest, sexiest, most arrogant man she'd ever known. A pity she didn't have time for a man.

Slowly he laid his cards on the table. Three queens and two tens. A full house.

Her smile was triumphant as she played her cards. Ace, king, queen, jack, and ten of hearts. A royal flush.

He conceded the game. Standing up, he removed his socks. Wadding them together, he tossed them into her lap.

"I've never been so thoroughly trounced at poker." He smiled down at her. "Tell me, Hannah, was it luck or did you cheat?"

"Do you think I'd tell and spoil a perfectly scandalous reputation?" Now that the game had ended, she felt vastly relieved. She'd won; she'd had her revenge, and best of all, the strip show was over. She tucked the socks into his jacket pocket and smiled at him. "By the way, Jim, you have nice legs."

"It's good to be loved." His hands went to the waistband of his briefs.

"Wait." She stood up and lifted his stack of clothes into her arms. "I've decided to be generous."

He inched the briefs down below his navel. "You won fair and square. I insist."

"No!"

"No?" He grinned. "Afraid my other body parts will be nice, too, Hannah?"

"You're impossible."

"It was your game." He slid the briefs down another inch.

For a moment Hannah was mesmerized by the dark swirl of hair on his flat stomach. She licked her dry lips as her gaze dropped lower. If he hadn't chuckled, she might have made a complete fool of herself, standing there imagining what he had in his briefs. Whoever had said revenge was sweet had never dealt with Jim Roman, she thought. Thoroughly aggravated at herself, she jerked her head up and glared at him.

"Keep the underwear. I don't think Greenville is ready for the sight of you naked." And neither was she. She whirled around and headed toward the door. His mocking laughter followed her through. She sailed across the empty room, bearing his clothes in front of her like a burnt offering. Her heart rate was up, and she felt flushed. Even the brush of his clothes against her skin made her tingle.

Her impetus carried her all the way to the parking lot. She leaned against her van and took several deep, steadying breaths. Lord, what that man did to her! Still holding his clothes, she lifted her face to the sky. It was navy blue velvet and lit with so many stars it looked like an artist's fantasy. A cool breeze fanned her hot face.

She'd give him three more minutes, she thought, three minutes to wonder how he was going to get across town in his underpants without being stopped by the cops and put in jail. That should teach him that she wasn't the kind of women he could pluck off the ground, plop onto a filly, and lead away like a child. She smiled. There was something to be said for his audacity.

She glanced down at her watch. He'd had time enough to worry about his predicament. Taking the armload of clothes, she started back toward the clubhouse.

"Going somewhere, Hannah?"

Jim appeared out of the darkness like a giant Greek god. A large white tablecloth was draped over his body, toga-style. For a moment she stood in the parking lot and stared. Never had she seen a man more magnificently suited to wear a toga. He looked even better than he had in his briefs.

"Good grief. Julius Caesar?"

"No. Mark Antony. I'm glad you waited, my serpent of old Nile." He didn't move; he simply stood there, a powerful man playing a powerful game.

She didn't know what bothered her the most—the way Jim Roman looked or the way he called her his serpent of old Nile, Antony's pet name for Cleopatra. Mark Antony and Cleopatra had been history's greatest lovers. They'd also been star-crossed, just as she and Jim were.

Her heart rate picked up speed as she faced him. Lovers. The word echoed through her mind. Even as she yearned for him, she denied her feelings. They weren't lovers; they never would be lovers. They were merely two gamblers who were fated for a casual mating. Unconsciously Hannah jutted her chin out. She was determined that was all they would be— casual bedfellows.

"You're very resourceful, Jim."

"I've always had to be."

Something in his tone made her look at his face. Behind the dashing smile was a vulnerable man. For the first time since they'd met, she wondered about his childhood. Her mother had described Jim's mother as "having had a hard time." She thought of her own happy, privileged childhood, and guilt slashed through her. She wondered if she'd carried her prank too far.

"I was on my way back with your clothes. I never meant to let you ride across town in your underwear." She held his clothes out to him.

To her surprise, he lifted her off the ground and spun around with her, laughing. "My beautiful wildcat, do you have any idea how appealing you are when you're repenting of your mischievous deeds?"

"I am *not* repenting. Put me down."

He held her aloft as easily as he would a doll. "What will you give me?"

She leaned toward him and practically purred, "Great pain if you don't."

"Woman, you drive an irresistible bargain." He set her on her feet but kept his hand on her waist. "Hannah, be nice to me. This is my last night here."

"So it is." The wedding was the next day, then Jim would be gone. Somehow she hadn't thought of him leaving so soon. He'd become so much a part of the family celebration, she'd been lulled into thinking he belonged in the Delta. But, of course, he didn't, she thought. He belonged in San Francisco as surely as she belonged in Glacier Bay.

She tipped her head back so she could look into his eyes. "How nice do you want me to be?"

"Go dancing with me."

"Dancing?"

He chuckled. "You had something else in mind?"

"Not in the parking lot."

His chuckle became an appreciative boom of laughter. "That's my Hannah, wicked to the very end." Taking her elbow, he led her toward his rented car.

"Aren't you going to change first?"

"No. I've grown fond of this toga. It lets in the breeze."

"Has our Mississippi heat been getting to you?"

His gaze stroked over her. "The heat, among other things." He opened her door and helped her inside.

"You're really serious about wearing that thing dancing?"

"I intend to have lots of fun watching you explain why you're dancing with a man wearing a tablecloth."

He drove to his favorite little dive by the waterfront. It was pleasantly smoky and uncrowded. Two couples sat in a corner booth holding hands, and one lone man occupied a barstool. The pianist glanced up and smiled, but never missed a beat.

The bartender called out a greeting as if seeing a man in a tablecloth toga was an everyday occurrence to him. "Glad you're back, Jim. Bourbon?"

"Not yet, Wayne. Have to dance with my lady." He took Hannah in his arms and began to dance.

"I'm no lady."

"How well I know." Pulling her closer, he pressed his cheek onto her hair. "Hmmm, nice. What is that fragrance you're wearing?"

"Lavender."

"The fragrance of ladies."

"What?"

"Nothing. You just jogged an old memory."

Hannah waited to see if he would elaborate, and when he didn't, she talked on. It helped keep her mind off the slow fire that was building in her. "When I'm on the job, I can never wear perfume. The sweet smell would attract too much attention. It's one of my small indulgences when I come home."

"Along with bubble baths?"

"How did you know?"

"It was a lucky guess. You stayed in that bathroom last night long enough to shrivel." He smiled down at her. "I'm so glad you didn't."

"You were listening?"

"At the door. Have you forgotten that I'm an eavesdropper?"

"I've forgotten nothing about you, Jim Roman."

"And I've forgotten nothing about you, Hannah Donovan." Nor was he likely to, he thought as they moved to the pulsing sensuous beat of the music. Blues would always remind him of this moment, with the Mississippi River whispering its secrets outside the window and Hannah Donovan working her magic in his arms. They were good together, just as he'd known they would be. She responded to the slightest pressure of his hand, her body moving in perfect rhythm with his.

He felt the tension building inside him until it was desire, full blown and heady. The woman in his arms had woven a spell around him, he decided, a spell that almost made him believe he could fall in love with a hellcat and settle down in some sleepy southern town. Or perhaps it was the town itself that had worked the magic. The languid pace of the days, the lack of noise and neon, and the quiet grace of the river had seduced him. He hadn't thought of crime in the last twenty-four hours nor had he felt his usual overwhelming need for frantic activity.

Hannah pulled back and tipped her face up to his. "You're so quiet. What are you thinking, Jim?"

"I'm thinking that I'll miss this little town." *And you*, he added to himself.

"This little town will miss you." *And so will I*, she thought. "We don't often get strangers dancing in tablecloth togas."

"Is that all they'll miss?"

"Yes," she lied. She moved her head back against his shoulder so she wouldn't see his charming, lop-sided half smile. She wouldn't allow herself to think of all the reasons for that vulnerable look on his face. She wouldn't allow herself to speculate about the man beneath that tough-warrior façade. She didn't want to know whether he'd ever loved or been loved, whether he'd ever been hurt, whether he'd ever been lonesome.

Dancing the way they were—so in tune they were almost one—was too much like being in love. And love had no place in her well-ordered life in the remote fjords of Alaska.

"I should go back," she said.

"One more dance, Hannah."

"Just one more."

It was well past midnight when they left the waterfront.

Hannah looked back at the cozy little place and

was filled with a sweet nostalgia. The tender way Jim had held her, the way his eyes had deepened when he'd looked at her, the way his voice had wrapped her in velvet—all came rushing over her. She hadn't allowed herself to feel so much in a long, long time. Maybe too long, she thought.

She wished she could press the evening and put it in a scrapbook.

Jim was unusually quiet as he drove her back to the country club for her van. It was a comfortable silence, and she discovered that she liked it. There was a great difference between the quietness of being alone and the quietness of a shared moment. In her cabin in Alaska she'd had years of being alone, and she'd always believed she wanted it that way. Now she wondered.

"I wish the evening could last forever, Hannah."

With a start she realized they were in the parking lot beside the clubhouse.

"You sound as if you really mean that, Jim."

"I do." He took her hand and lifted it to his lips. "I've discovered that romancing you is just as much fun as sparring with you."

Her breath caught at his choice of words. "Was it romance?"

With one arm he pulled her close, so close she could feel his warm breath against her temple. She saw the sparks ignite in his eyes. He was going to kiss her. She could almost taste his lips on hers.

"It might have been—" Abruptly he stopped speaking and pulled back from her. She felt the distance he put between them. "It might have been," he repeated, "if you were the girl of my dreams."

Was it hope that shriveled inside her at his words? Don't be ridiculous, she chided herself.

"How fortunate for both of us that I'm not." She jerked open the car door and plunged out into the night.

"Hannah. Hannah! Wait!"

She ignored his calls. She probably should turn around and thank him. For a giddy, foolish moment she'd been dangerously close to making the same mistake she'd made with Rai.

She slammed the door of her van and revved the engine. The tired old motor sounded like a polar bear with a toothache and was loud enough to wake everybody in Greenville, but she didn't care. She just wanted to be home and out of Jim Roman's sight.

By the time she got home, she'd cooled off enough to think straight. What she needed was to forget about the unexpected glow Jim Roman lit inside her and to follow through with her original plan—seduce him and forget him. Once and for all she needed to prove to herself that she was in charge of her life and that no man could ever take that from her again.

Although the air-conditioning was running full force, she felt the need for some fresh air. She opened her bedroom window and sat on the windowsill, leaning out so she could breathe the night air and glimpse the stars. The peace of the evening was in direct contrast to the turmoil inside her. *Ahhh, Jim,* she whispered, *why do you make me feel this way?*

Far in the distance she heard the sounds of a car. He was coming. The moonlight lent a magic to the moment so that the dusty rented car seemed to be a glorious chariot and Jim a mighty warrior returning from battle. Hannah leaned farther out the window to get a better view.

Jim still wore the toga with the air of a man who didn't care what the rest of the world thought. As she watched, he absently patted his hips, then reached inside the car and pulled out a pipe. She had never seen him smoke. Her brother Paul had once told her that he smoked his pipe only when he needed to do some serious thinking. What was Jim thinking, she wondered. Was he shaken by the same feelings that raged through her? Was he replaying every kiss, every touch, every look they'd shared, just as she was? She envied him his pipe. It gave him something solid to hold on to.

Hannah stayed at the window until Jim started toward the house and disappeared under the eave of the front porch. She imagined the way the front door creaked when he came through, imagined the way he would be moving quietly so he wouldn't wake the rest of the household. Her heart hammered as she listened for that one squeaky board at the top of the stairs that would betray him.

When she heard it, her resolve firmed. She'd give him five minutes, she decided, then she'd make her move.

Jim was standing at the window, looking out, when she opened the door that connected his bedroom to the bath they shared. He turned at the sound of her entrance.

She stood just inside the door in a patch of moonlight. With her swirling red dress and her tumbled dark hair she looked like fire and smoke, he thought. He didn't smile, didn't speak, merely stood watching her. Hot, dangerous, wild, exciting—all the things she was washed over him.

"I knew you'd come." He watched the effect of his statement on her. She remained in the doorway, composed and serene.

"You give yourself too much credit."

Her tart reply made him smile. *Sweet* would never be the word to describe Hannah. "You're not here because of my irresistible charm?"

"I'm not even here because of your refreshing arrogance."

The offhand compliment pleased him. "Do you find me refreshing, Hannah."

"Invigorating probably would be a better word. Being with you is like taking a cold dip in Glacier Bay."

"Come closer, Hannah. I have a way to heat the waters."

She seemed to float toward him, borne along on the billowing red cloud of a dress and a wave of heady fragrance. Passion ripped through him with a suddenness that made him almost dizzy. He'd never known a woman's walk could do that to a man.

She stopped inches away from him. With her index finger she reached out and skimmed his cheek. He didn't move. He barely breathed as her finger moved slowly downward, across his throat and into the mat of chest hair exposed by his makeshift toga.

"That's what I'm counting on, West Coast Warrior."

The blues music of her voice hummed through him, tensing his already tight muscles. He hadn't meant to be bewitched by her.

He caught the hand that played along his chest. Lifting it, palm up, to his lips, he sucked, trying to ease his hot aching by drinking in the coolness of her. He heard her catch her breath.

"Do you like that, Hannah?"

"Skilled lips always excite me."

"Do you want more?"

"Yes."

He gathered her into his embrace and took her lips. She was willing and pliant, fiery and passionate. She was all the things he'd ever wanted in a woman except one: She was not and never would be a woman he could take care of. Hannah Donovan was the most strongly independent woman he'd ever met. And the most exciting.

Heat seemed to steam up from them as they kissed. The term "burning passion" took on new meaning for him. He was on fire with need, sizzling, scorching with desire. He wanted to rip her dress away and plunge mindlessly into her. And yet . . . His thoughts spun away, and he groaned. Sweet. Her lips were so sweet.

"Hannah. My Hannah." He was scarcely aware that he'd spoken, was scarcely aware that he was moving his hands over her body as if she were something precious.

"Hmmm . . ." she whispered, "you are . . . delicious. I can't . . . get enough."

Nor can I, he thought, *Nor will I ever.* With sudden clarity he realized that nothing would ever be casual between them. What had started as a challenge had turned into something else entirely, something he didn't want to name, something he didn't want to think about. More to the point, he realized he couldn't take Hannah this way.

Recklessly he took one last deep drink from her lips, then he broke the kiss and gazed down at her. With her wide indigo eyes and her tumbled jet hair, she was desirable almost beyond imagining. He nearly changed his mind.

"Jim?"

"Did I succeed in making things hot for you?"

His words hit Hannah like a dash of ice water. She raked her hands through her hair and tried to decide what had happened. One minute she'd been in charge and the next she'd been lost. All it had taken was one look, one touch from Jim.

She drew a shaky breath. The game she was playing had taken a dangerous turn. With great certainty she realized that Jim's bed would never be a proving ground of her independence. She didn't want to think about what it would have been: She merely wanted to hang on to the few shreds of control she still possessed.

Without taking her eyes off his, she reached out and loosened the knot that held his makeshift toga in place.

"Not hot enough." When she peeled the tablecloth from his body, she managed to look both cool and wickedly desirable. She'd have been pleased if she had known what a struggle Jim had to keep his hands off her.

"Not nearly hot enough," she added as she ran her hands over his chest.

A shaft of moonlight caught the flames that sprang into his eyes as her hands moved downward. With her index finger she lightly traced across the front of this briefs.

His sharp intake of breath made her smile. "Do you like that?" she asked softly.

"Be careful how you play with fire. You might get burned."

"I'm a big girl now, Jim. I know what I'm doing."

"Do you, Hannah?"

Something in his voice made her hesitate. Her finger stopped its erotic journey as she looked into his face. It was tight with an emotion that looked almost like anger.

"Do you?" he repeated.

She tossed back her hair and jutted out her chin. "Yes. I know that you want me."

His majestic silence filled the room. Hannah's breath caught in her throat as she looked at him.

"I've made you want me," she whispered.

"Yes."

That was all she had, that one word, but it was satisfaction enough. It was time to end the game while she still could.

"You said I'd come to you, and I did . . ." She took a step back. "What you didn't know was that I would walk away—untouched."

Willing herself not to run, she turned and walked slowly to the door. She expected some challenge from him, or at least mocking laughter, but there was nothing except a screaming silence.

Keep going, she told herself. *Don't turn around.*

She made it to her bedroom before she looked back. And then all she could see was the darkness that separated them.

Jacob arrived with the morning.

Hannah was the first to see him. Unable to sleep, she'd risen with the sun, put on her jogging shorts, and started outside for a good, hard run. Just as she reached the front porch, Graves Johnson's station wagon stopped in the driveway and out stepped her youngest brother.

She raced toward him, "Jacob!"

He grabbed her with one arm and waved good-bye to their longtime neighbor with the other. "Thanks for the lift, Johnson."

"Glad to do it, Jacob."

Hannah caught Jacob's face between her hands. "Let me look at you." Jacob was smaller than the rest of the Donovan men, but he managed to look every bit as big. He was compact and powerful, with the bright red hair of his mother's Scottish ancestors, Hannah's vivid blue eyes, and a rakish grin all his own.

Hannah tenderly brushed a lock of hair off his forehead. "You've no right to look so wonderful. It's been almost a year."

"There's a big world out there to see." Jacob turned his face toward the city and got a faraway look in his eyes. "How is she?"

"Rachel?" Hannah need not have asked. She knew Jacob was inquiring about the woman who had jilted him. "Happy, according to the Greenville grapevine. She and her husband are living in Seattle now, I believe."

"Seattle. So far away." The fleeting look that crossed his face might have been pain, but with Jacob, Hannah was never sure. He'd always been a great pretender. The family prankster, the vagabond, the one who made the rest of them laugh.

He made her laugh now. Affecting a frown, he lifted a strand of her hair. "Is that gray I see? Thirty and not married. What will Aunt Agnes say?"

"Plenty. Just wait until she gets hold of you. You're not a spring chicken anymore, yourself, baby brother."

"I can handle Aunt Agnes. I'll just invite her to go hang gliding. She'll be too scared to give advice."

Hannah roared with laughter. "Remember that Christmas you took her up in your balloon? She gave Pop hell for months about raising such a daredevil."

"It wasn't half as bad as the tangent she went on when she caught you out behind the barn smoking a pipe."

A brief image of Jim with his pipe came to her mind. She firmly pushed it aside. "I never did get the hang of that." Hannah squeezed his hand. "Why didn't you let us know you were coming? How did you come anyway? Your Cessna? Your balloon?"

"Learjet. Mine. Johnson's flight came in right after I landed, and he gave me a lift. I didn't want to wake anybody this early. Especially not Hallie. They say a bride needs her beauty sleep."

"I wouldn't know."

"Neither would I."

They looked at each other in the early dawn, a brother and sister whose special bond needed no words. Finally Jacob spoke.

"What does one do on his sister's wedding day, Hannah?"

She glanced upward toward Jim's window, then turned back to her brother. "Run like hell."

"My sentiments exactly."

Jacob tossed his duffel bag onto the porch, then the two of them sprinted down the driveway, turned east, and raced into the sun.

Six

Hallie's wedding was at two o'clock in the afternoon.

Jim sat in the back of the church, watching. The bride was beautiful, the groom was handsome, and everybody looked happy. It was an occasion of great joy, but he felt like hell. Standing at the front of the church was the reason—Hannah Donovan. With her madonna smile and her sedate lace and pearls, she almost made him believe she wasn't the same sultry woman who'd come to his room the previous night and finished destroying every dream he'd ever had about a sweet old-fasioned girl.

"Do you take this woman . . ."

The minister's voice penetrated Jim's consciousness. *Do you take this woman?* His gaze burned over Hannah. Yes, he thought, he'd take that woman. He'd take her in the pasture behind her house, in the hayloft, in her bed, in his bed. He'd take her anywhere he could get her. He'd even take her to San Francisco if she'd come. But then what? She was as wedded to her career in that godforsaken wilderness as he was to his in the big city.

". . . Will you love her and cherish her, honor and keep her, till death do you part. . . ."

Who was he kidding? Jim mocked himself. He could no more have a future with that wildcat than he could stop breathing. With him and Hannah, it would be till the next assignment do us part or the next job in Sri Lanka. Hell, it might even be till the next boat out of the harbor. Who knew? He could turn out to be just like his old man. It was best to catch his four o'clock plane out of Greenville and never look back.

He managed not to cross paths with Hannah during the reception back at the Donovan home. He considered that he was getting pretty good at avoiding her. He'd managed it ever since the gut-ripping confrontation of the night before. Standing in the library with the celebrating Donovans milling about, he glanced down at his watch. Almost time to leave. He'd thank Anna and Matthew for the hospitality, then be on his way.

He made it all the way up to his bedroom. His hand was on his bag when he heard her voice.

"Leaving without saying good-bye, Jim?"

Joy surged through him, then panic, then a great sense of destiny. Turning slowly, he saw Hannah. She was standing in the doorway, still wearing lace and pearls.

"You look good enough to eat." He crossed the room in three quick strides, pulled her into his arms, and shut the door. He could feel her heart hammering against his chest. "And I plan to."

"Is that a challenge?" Her hands skimmed his face.

He tipped her chin up with a forefinger and looked

deep into her eyes. He had to taste her one last time, even if it meant missing his plane. "No, it's a promise."

They came together with the wild hunger of two people who had lived too long with denial. He hauled her hips into his, seeking to ease his passion by fitting himself into her soft hollows. He could feel the heat of her through their clothes. He groaned as his lips took hers.

Theirs was no gentle joining. It was the thunder of a storm on the Pacific; it was the roar of a glacier splitting and plunging into the bay; it was the explosion of a million stars burning through the night.

They kissed until their lips felt bruised. Jim was the one to pull away.

"If only there were time enough," he whispered.,

"There will never be time for us."

"No," he agreed. "You'll be going back to Glacier Bay?"

"Yes. In two weeks. And you to San Francisco."

He nodded. "You'll have your marine research."

"And you'll have your battles with crime."

"Always."

"It's best. Men complicate my life."

His smile was crooked. "Even fierce West Coast Warriors?"

"Especially warriors."

"Then it's good that I'm leaving." Slowly he traced her face with his hand, memorizing every contour. "Independent women with smoky blue eyes and stormcloud hair complicate mine."

"We would have been good together, Jim."

"Thunder and lightning always are." He longed for one last desperate kiss, but he knew if he tasted her lips once more, he might never leave. He released her. "Good-bye, Hannah." From somewhere deep inside he summoned up a magnificient indifference to combat his passion. "Come out to San Francisco to see me—any Thursday. That's my day off."

Without giving her time to reply, he picked up his bag and hurried from the room. He never looked back.

Hannah caught the doorknob for support as she watched him walk out of her life. It's best, she told herself. She'd known that when she came up the stairs. The night before she'd gone to him to prove her independence, and now she'd come to him to prove . . . Her mind groped for the right answer. Independence again? Not likely. She was too honest to accept that lie, even from herself. The plain and simple truth was that she'd gotten exactly what she'd come for—a mind-shattering, resolve-shaking, heart-thundering kiss.

It was over, and she was walking away untouched. She'd keep telling herself that until she believed it. Hannah squared her shoulders, jutted out her chin, and walked downstairs to join her family.

"I've never seen you so restless."

For a moment Jim didn't reply. He stood at the window of John Searles's Pacific Heights home, which overlooked the majestic panorama of San Francisco. Everything was clean and beautiful, shaded with the perpetual mist that hung over the city, from the opulent homes that nestled into the hills all the way down to the sleek boats in the bay. He was glad to be back.

"It's this damned inactivity," he finally said, turning from the window to face his publisher. "When are you going to turn me loose on the bastards that are turning our kids into junkies and our streets into a jungle?"

"It's too soon."

"Too soon! It's been six weeks." He crammed his hands into his pockets and paced the polished marble floor. "I feel like some damned hothouse flower. Covering the doings of the jet set all over the country is not my idea of investigative reporting."

"Take a look at this, Jim. It came this morning."

Jim glanced from John to the flat brown envelope that lay on the chrome and glass table. He recognized the scrawl, done in red ink, that snaked boldly across the envelope.

"The same people?"

"Yes. Same type stationery, same phrasing. No outright threats, but pointing clearly enough to you this time that we can go to the police."

"No police. If I have to have cops wet-nurse me every time I step on somebody's toes, I might as well turn in my typewriter."

John picked the envelope up and handed it to him. "I think you should read it before you make that decision."

Jim ripped the letter out of the envelope. It was the same as all the others he'd received, a crude poem handwritten on unlined dime-store paper.

"The mighty warrior drew his bow and shot into the night. The arrow turned, came back to him, and gave him quite a fright. It ripped into his floating house, trailing streams of fire. It ripped into his blackguard heart, branding him a liar."

Jim wadded the paper into a ball and tossed it back onto the table. John's suntanned face was unreadable as he smoothed the paper and stuffed it back into the envelope.

"This one is worse than the other two, Jim."

"I'll concede that, but I'll be damned if I'll request protection."

"From a very practical standpoint, I think we can ask the police to beef up the patrol along the waterfront." John pulled off his glasses and tapped the frames against the brown envelope. "This floating house is obviously your houseboat. It sounds like they mean to torch it."

"Most cowardly deeds are done at night. I'll ask Colter to help me keep a lookout. His boat is in the slip next to mine."

"Hmmm." John closed his eyes and leaned back.

Jim was familiar with that nonanswer. It always meant that John Searles was thinking, and that when he had finished, he'd do exactly as he pleased, no matter what anyone else thought about the matter. Their clashes had been titanic and legendary around the publishing office, for John's stubbornness matched his own. That was the first thing Jim had noticed when he'd come to work for him eight years before, that and his age. He was barely three years older than Jim, but he looked ten years younger. Wealth does that, Jim mused. It cushions the shocks of real life.

Jim waited. Only one thing was certain: Whatever was decided today would not affect their relationship. The respect they held for each other more than balanced their tempers.

"This is what we'll do." John flashed his pleased,

boyish smile as he looked up. "I'll arrange for extra security around the waterfront—a private company—and you'll go to Texas."

"So . . . you're going to send me into hiding again?"

"Yes. You did quite well with that Donovan wedding assignment in Greenville. And those pieces you did in Charleston and Savannah were superb. I thought I'd send you out to Houston to cover the opening of a new multimillion-dollar spa. It's called The Magic Touch, and it will be crawling with celebrities. The story will make a nice addition to *America's Elite*."

"That Donovan assignment was more dangerous than a firing squad. I would have been safer in San Francisco."

"What?"

"Nothing. Just reminiscing." Cramming his hand into his pockets, Jim turned toward the window that looked out over his beloved city. Hannah's image filled his mind. He saw her as clearly as he had six weeks earlier, her red dress billowing, her dark hair tumbled. Fire and smoke. And he'd been burned. The only cure would be to step into the fire again.

Resolutely he turned to face his publisher. "I have a counterproposal."

"I'm listening."

The commuter plane began its descent toward Glacier Bay.

Jim, who'd always thought San Francisco was God's gift to mankind, found himself holding his breath over the grandeur of the scene below him. Enormous mountains capped with snow and shrouded with mists presided with ancient majesty over the lush forest of spruce and hemlock. Gleaming pinnacles of ice rose up from the water, tips of the glaciers that guarded the ends of the fjords. As the small plane dipped lower, he could see bright ribbons of color, patches of yellow dryas and strips of scarlet fireweed, wildflowers he'd read about in the guidebook to Alaska.

A saying of the Hoonah Indians, Glacier Bay's ancestral people, came to his mind: "God dwells here." Jim thought that surely must be so, for the land was like a benediction.

Almost reluctantly he leaned toward the man in the seat next to him, a crusty old-timer who had boarded in Juneau for the twenty-minute flight to Gustavus. "Did you say you know Dr. Hannah Donovan?"

The man, who called himself Sleddog, shifted his wad of chewing tobacco from one side of his mouth to the other. "Yep."

He didn't talk much—except about himself. After he'd boarded the plane and introduced himself, he'd talked for three minutes nonstop about how he'd gotten his name. It seemed he knew more about sledding than any old dog in Alaska. Jim resigned himself to a conversation that was equivalent to extracting teeth.

"Can you give me directions to her house?"

The old man cackled. "It ain't much of a house."

"But you know where it is?"

"Everybody does. She's famous in these parts."

"For her research?"

His high-pitched cackling laughter sounded again. "You done tickled my fancy, young feller. Ain't nobody around here understands all that whale mumbo-jumbo. Whales've been here since God created Alaska, and they'll be here when you and me's turning up daisies. Naah, Hannah Donovan is famous because every year she beats the socks off the men in the Yukon Quest."

Jim felt the jolt as the plane touched tarmac. He decided the old man would be useless as a guide. Briefly he regretted not phoning ahead and letting Hannah know he was coming. He grinned as he thought of her reaction to that news. She probably would have met him with her .300 Magnum, if she'd met him at all.

No, he thought as he picked up his gear and started to the small terminal, it was best to surprise her.

"Hey, wait up, young feller." The old man touched his elbow. A stiff breeze had caused his sparse hair to stand up like white cream puffs around his head. "You wanting to go to Hannah Donovan's or not?"

"Yes, I am."

"Then you'd best load your gear into my pickup truck. Ain't many folks around here who'll venture over them rough backroads all the way up to where she lives."

"How far?"

"Oh, up past Bartlett Cove, 'bout thirty, forty miles, give or take a few."

Jim tossed his duffel bag into the back end of a 1955 Chevrolet pickup that didn't look as though it would get to the next corner on greased wheels, let alone forty miles on rough backroads. He thought briefly of his fool's errand and decided the shakeup would do him good. Maybe it would jar his brain back into place.

Carefully he stowed the carton containing his type-writer and other writing essentials in the back, then climbed into the pickup.

Conversation was limited by the jarring drive. That was all right with Jim. It gave him time to decide what in the hell he was going to say when he saw Dr. Hannah Donovan.

Hannah leaned over the boat railing and watched as the graceful humpback exploded from the bay, spreading its flippers for a splashdown. Bopeep was back, she thought. She recognized him by the pattern of white on his underside and by the left flipper that was shaped somewhat like the crook of a shepherd's staff. She made rapid notations in her record book. Bopeep had not been sighted in these waters in two years. She'd feared that he had fallen prey to the whale poachers.

Suddenly the haunting song of the humpback echoed from out of the deep. Goose bumps rose on Hannah's arms, and she quickly swung her gaze to her recorder, double-checking that it would be capturing the rare and beautiful music of the whale. Leaning farther over the railing, she listened. The song became fainter as Bopeep sounded. Eventually it ceased altogether, for the whale either had gone too deep to be heard or had stopped singing.

Hannah glanced at her watch. Six P.M. She'd meant to leave her vigil at six and head north toward the small building that housed the North Pacific Institute of Oceanographic Research, but she decided that further sightings of Bopeep were more important than catching up on the paperwork that awaited her at the institute.

She stayed out four more hours, taking advantage of the summer light that made night nearly indistinguishable from day. Then, drawing her wool parka close to combat the chill, she turned her boat toward shore.

The minute she caught sight of her cabin she knew something was wrong. But in the misty evening light, everything looked the same—the heavy log door was shut, the tiny white maiden flowers along the path were untrampled, the dogs were quiet in the kennels. When Pete rose from the front porch to greet her, she dismissed her suspicions as foolish. She'd done lots of foolish things since her sister's wedding in Greenville, she thought as she patted her dog's head, and she'd placed the blame squarely on Jim Roman.

Hannah pushed open her cabin door, and there he was, the West Coast Warrior, tipped back in one of her cane-bottom chairs, looking as if he owned the whole place. His typewriter was set up on her wooden table, his duffel bag was on the floor, and his coat was tossed over the coat rack.

She stood in the doorway, transfixed. A part of her wanted him to be a figment of her imagination, and a part of her wanted to rush forward and throw herself into his arms.

"Hello, Hannah." His smile was just as devilish as she had remembered, and every bit as devastating.

"How did you get in?"

"I'm an expert at getting into places that would keep me out."

"How did you get past my dogs?" She tried to look

as severe as possible and hoped he didn't see her hands trembling.

"I charmed them."

"You're trespassing."

Jim rose from the chair and slowly stalked her. "Where are your southern manners, Hannah? Is that any way to treat a guest in your home?"

"Don't you come a step closer."

He never slowed his pace. "What's the matter, wildcat? Afraid I'll kiss you or afraid I won't?"

"Why, you arrogant jackass."

"Still the same old Hannah." He chuckled. "How reassuring to know that some things never change." He lifted her face with his finger. "Aren't you even going to say hello?"

The exhilaration she'd felt at sighting Bopeep was nothing compared to the gale of excitement that swept over her now. All the old doubts she'd felt in Greenville began to come back. Or had they ever left in the first place, she wondered as she looked at the familiar face that had haunted her dreams for six weeks.

"Why are you here?"

Instead of answering, he traced her face with one finger as if he were trying to make himself believe that she was real.

"Why?" she whispered.

"Not to play games."

His hands lingered over her lips, circling slowly, while her heart tried to beat its way out of her chest. When the questing hand moved on to her cheek, she took a deep, shaky breath.

"Why did you come all the way to Glacier Bay, Jim?"

He shoved his hands into his pockets and moved back to the chair by the fireplace. "I'm on assignment. I'm going to write a series of stories on your work here."

"Surely not for *America's Elite*."

"No. You and I don't fall into that category, do we, Hannah?"

"Hardly." Now that he was safely on the other side of the room, she felt that she could move. She peeled off her parka and began to putter around in the small cooking alcove. It would be best to look his way as little as possible.

"What category would you say we fall into? Lovers?"

She felt as if somebody had socked her in the stomach. Jerking her head around, she stared at him, then she wished she hadn't. He looked too cocky, too handsome, and altogether too desirable. "We didn't . . ."

"No, we didn't, but we will."

"I thought you said you didn't come to play games."

He tried to look contrite and failed. "I didn't. This trip is strictly business. I'm here to do a series for *Untamed America*."

"I always welcome a story on our work at the institute. The more people who know the plight of the whales, the better." She held a shaker over the halibut she planned to have for dinner, then realized she'd already coated it with herbs. "My only regret is that John Searles didn't send another writer."

"You like variety, do you, Hannah?"

"Yes." She was going to learn a lot about the art of lying while Jim was there, she thought as she slammed her dinner into the oven and leaned against the counter. "But since you're here, we'll make the best of it. You can stay here for the night. Tomorrow I'll try to arrange other accommodations for you. There'a a lovely lodge in Bartlett Cove."

"The present arrangement is to my liking."

"You can't stay here."

"Why not?" When she didn't answer, he asked again, softer, "Why not, Hannah?"

"Because . . . I don't like distractions in my work."

"Then I can stay in Bartlett Cove." He'd agreed with her much too easily, she decided. Somehow that didn't reassure her. Furthermore, when he reached into his pocket and casually pulled out his pipe, he reminded her of a lion—a hungry lion. Even his smile was predatory. "However," he continued, taking a slow drag on his pipe, "it will slow your work down considerably, waiting for me to make that long, bumpy ride and that incredible mountain-goat trek back to your cabin every day. I can hardly report on your work without seeing it firsthand. No"—he paused, taking a long drag on his pipe—"I think it will be best if I stay here."

Unconsciously Hannah glanced up toward her sleeping loft. Across the room Jim chuckled. "Worried, wildcat?"

She tossed her head. "Not in the least. I've handled everything from a maverick wolverine to a rampaging bull moose. I certainly can handle you."

Jim roared with laughter. "I would have been disappointed if you'd said otherwise." When his laughter ceased, he grew very still. "I've missed you, Hannah," he said quietly. "Lord knows I tried not to, but I missed you anyway."

"And I've missed you . . ." Hannah was spellbound by his eyes. *Don't look at me like that*, she thought.

The delicious aroma of baking halibut and the heat of Jim's passion filled the cabin. She didn't know what she would have done if her quirky sense of humor hadn't saved her. Suddenly she thought of herself, seated in a fancy restaurant, smelling halibut and getting hot for Jim. She'd have Pavlov's salivating dog beat by a mile. She shook herself out of her reverie and finished what she'd started to say. "But not enough to make a fool of myself." She turned her attention to the baking fish. "Do make yourself at home. There's no reason in the world why we can't each go about our usual business for the duration of this assignment."

"None whatsoever."

Jim tamped out his pipe and moved across the room, driven by his need to be near Hannah. When he reached the small cooking alcove, he moved in and leaned over her shoulder, close enough to inhale her fragrance. She smelled like wind and sunshine.

"Is that fish I smell?" He took a deep breath, pretending to be sniffing the dinner, and a silky strand of her hair brushed against his cheek. He felt as if he'd been branded. "I thought you didn't cook, Hannah."

"Halibut is my one and only specialty. One can hardly survive without—" She went very still as his hands cupped her shoulders. Slowly he turned her in his arms.

"One can hardly survive without touching you, Hannah." His hands caressed her shoulders and moved up the back of her neck. Tiny sparks lit the center of his eyes as he watched her sable hair drift through his fingers. "Do you know that I spent two hours one day thinking of the way your hair felt against my skin?" He twirled a long lock around his finger. "It was one of my better days."

"Why are you here, Jim?"

"Don't you know?"

She closed her eyes, and when she opened them, Jim felt as if he were gazing into the sun. "Yes, I know."

"I'm here because I couldn't stay away."

Hannah reached up and gently traced the scar on his forehead. "How shall we start this time, Jim?"

Now that he was there, he'd be damned if he knew. He'd tracked her all the way to the Alaskan wilds with no other thought than to hold her in his arms one more time and purge her from his system. He wanted her. There was no doubt about that. He wanted her as he'd wanted no other woman. And that very obsession scared the hell out of him.

"Why don't we start with a kiss, Hannah, and then we'll go on to the halibut?"

Hannah laughed, and as she did, she felt the tension ease out of her. She'd survived one invasion by the West Coast Warrior, she thought. There was no reason she couldn't survive two.

"Are you asking this time, Jim?"

"Yes. You once told me you like to be asked."

"Only if it's the right man who's doing the asking."

"Am I the right man?"

Her lips told him what he wanted to know. They spoke the same wild and hungry language as his own.

She tasted of the sea and of wildflowers. And as he kissed her, he knew he would never get enough. Groaning, he pulled her closer. She was both satin and steel. Her slim, athletic body was softened by enticing curves and inviting hollows. In six weeks time he'd forgotten how a woman's body could make him lose his mind. Hannah, his mind whispered. Only Hannah.

She melted into him, pressed so close that she wasn't sure whether the hammering against her chest was Jim's heart or her own. And she didn't care. She was in Jim's arms and that's all that mattered at the moment. Tomorrow would have to take care of itself.

He lifted his mouth from hers, and she felt deprived. "It's been so long, Hannah."

"Too long," she said softly.

His lips brushed across hers, then wandered down her throat until they were pressed in the hollow where her pulse beat like the wings of a frightened bird.

"I'm so hungry." His tongue did magic things to her throat. "So hungry," he murmured as his mouth moved lower.

"The halibut . . ."

"Can wait."

Seven

Jim had his hands on the buttons of her shirt before he came to his senses. Taking Hannah now would not be release: It would be bondage. It would also be foolish. Nothing had changed between them. There in her sparsely furnished, primitive, functional cabin, he was more aware than ever that Dr. Hannah Donovan was a dedicated professional. He wanted more. He wanted a soft, yielding woman who would be completely his, one who would be content to remain at his side, always. He wanted a woman whose mind was on children not whales. He wanted a woman he could take care of in the manner in which Brick Roman should have cared for the woman he'd married.

Pulling back, he crammed his hands into his pockets. "That was a nice appetizer. Now I'm ready for the main course."

"The main course?"

He crooked one eyebrow upward. "Halibut—unless you have something else in mind."

She put her hands on her hips. Her face was alight with magnificent rage. "What I have in mind is taking my gun to you, Jim Roman, and sending you back to San Francisco, where you belong."

Bravo, Hannah, he thought. He loved her fiery spirit. "You're right. I do belong there—just as you belong here." He turned toward her cabinets and began to rummage. "Where do you keep the dishes? I'll set the table."

"On your right, above the sink." She opened the oven and took out the halibut. "Let's get a few things straight: I won't cook for you, I won't pick up after you, I won't change my schedule for you, and most of all, I won't kiss you. I rise early and work late. If you want a story, you'll have to keep pace with me." She slammed the halibut on the table with the outraged vigor of a woman spurned.

"Do you do laundry?"

"I certainly do not.

"I didn't think so, but then a woman of your talents doesn't have to do laundry." Feeling only a small twinge of guilt at the way he was protecting both of them from their attraction to each other, he chuckled as she rose to the bait.

"And that's another thing. I won't share my *talents*, as you so shamelessly call them, with you."

"It takes two to kiss, wildcat."

"I made one mistake—long ago. I won't repeat it."

He was stunned at the black jealousy that ripped his gut. At that moment he hated Rai Ghayami as intensely as he'd ever hated any man. The dishes clattered to the table as he strode over and cupped her face, forcing her to look into his eyes. "No man stands between me and what I want, Hannah. No man."

"And what it is you want, West Coast Warrior?" The fire in her eyes challenged him.

At that moment even he didn't know. He conceded the victory to Hannah. "Dinner. Then bed."

"I'll share my dinner, but I won't share my bed."

"It's inevitable, Hannah." His thumbs caressed her cheeks before he let her go.

"Never."

Seeing the indomitable Hannah in her glorious moment of triumph made the trip from San Francisco worthwhile, he thought. She'd generated more excitement in half an hour than all the silly, artificial women he'd dated in the last six weeks.

Finally he knew why he'd come to Glacier Bay: He was addicted to Hannah Donovan. How in the hell he could ever reconcile that to his addiction to the big city and to his search for a dream woman, he didn't know.

"Fish is getting cold," he said. "Let's eat."

"Eating on an angry stomach is bad for the digestion."

"Shall we kiss and make up?"

"You blackguard." Hannah could tell by the way he was grinning that he was no longer serious. Their skirmish was over, and she'd won. "Don't you ever behave?"

"Rarely."

"How well I know."

They sat down to the halibut and a salad Hannah pulled from the refrigerator. Jim silently applauded as Hannah made the transition from enraged female to perfect hostess.

"Jim, how long do you expect this story to take?"

"A few days."

"I want the story to be great."

"So do I."

"Then shall we put our personal feelings aside—for the good of the institute and the good of your story?"

Could he, he wondered. Could he concentrate on anything except the magnificent woman sitting across the table? He had to; he knew that. For both their sakes, he had to.

He smiled. "You strike a hard bargain, lady, but you're on."

After dinner Hannah began to prepare immediately for bed. In order to make the most of her day, she got up early, she'd explained to Jim. That meant early to bed.

He listened to the sounds of her in the shower. There was hardly any way he could do otherwise, since the cabin was so small. The sound of the water tightened his already jangling nerves. It didn't take much imagination to picture Hannah, her trim body gleaming with moisture and slick with soap. To combat his own increasing passion, he unpacked his faithful Remington, rolled paper into the machine, and began to type. The tapping of the typewriter keys soothed him, as it always did. The pleasure of seeing his thoughts transform a blank sheet of paper into something akin to a manuscript filled him with joy. He pitied the poor fools who had been wooed away by that electronic, whirring monster—the word processor. Let them get eyestrain from looking at the phosphorescent screen. He'd stick to the old ways.

When Hannah came out of the bathroom, his fingers went still and his thoughts scattered like frightened mice. Her hair was wet, slicked back, as black and shiny as the pelt of a seal. There was not a trace of makeup on her face, but she was still as vivid as a poppy. Standing almost shyly in the bathroom doorway, wearing a red terry-cloth robe, she was the most magnificently gorgeous creature he'd ever seen.

He cleared away the sudden frog in his throat. "Finished already? Judging from your bathing habits in Greenville, I expected you to be in there at least an hour."

"You can't take a bubble bath in a shower." She moved across the room with that grace that had captured his imagination—if not his heart—in Greenville. When she leaned over his shoulder, he caught a whiff of her. She smelled like flower-scented soap and herbal shampoo—a heady combination.

"What are you working on?"

"A little background for the story. Will the typing bother you?"

"No. As a matter of fact, I find the sound soothing, like rain against the roof."

"Good. I'll work awhile, then."

"Well . . . good night, Jim."

"Good night, Hannah."

Although he turned back to his typing, he was aware of every movement she made as she prepared for bed. When her robe hit the loft floor with a soft plunk, desire punched him in the gut so hard, he had to clamp his teeth shut to keep from groaning aloud. The squeaking of her bedsprings almost did him in. He nearly bolted from the cabin. Sleddog had told him there were bears in the woods, but at the moment he'd rather face a grizzly than face a night sleeping in the same room with Hannah Donovan.

Jim gritted his teeth and kept on typing.

She'd lied, Hannah thought, as she lay wide-eyed in her bed, gazing through the skylight at the strange summer glow of night. Every tap of the typewriter keys reminded her that Jim Roman was in the room. He'd invaded her sanctuary, her haven, her workplace. What was worse, he'd invaded her heart. When he'd stalked her in the kitchen and taken her in his arms, she'd known she was fighting a losing battle. She'd no more remained untouched in Greenville than she could fly to the moon without a rocket. He'd touched her: He'd awakened her passion, stirred her imagination, and . . . yes, she had to admit the truth, he'd even touched her heart.

She clenched her hands into fists and willed herself not to toss and turn. Damn him, damn him. Why did he have to come back? Just when she was getting everything back under control, why did the West Coast Warrior have to invade her senses? She didn't want to lose control.

The truth bolted through her with a force that almost shot her out of the bed. That was it, she thought. All the while she'd been saying that her career was hard and demanding and left no room for a man, much less a family; all the while she'd been blaming her one ill-fated affair with Rai, she'd been hiding the truth, even from herself. She was afraid. She was scared to death to relinquish control of even one little part of her life to somebody else.

"Hannah loves to be in charge. Hannah loves to boss things." She almost could hear the loving voices of her family. What they didn't know was that the woman who had faced down a rampaging bull moose and a giant grizzly was afraid of a little thing called love. Why, she asked herself. Her parents and her brothers had beautiful marriages. Why should love scare the hell out of her?

Staring up through the skylight, she had another revelation. Hallie. All their lives the twins had had similar experiences. They skinned their knees at the same time even though they were on different sides of town; they had appendectomies together; they both made the high school debating team; they both won scholarships to college. Hallie's first experience at love and marriage had been a disaster. Although Hannah wasn't superstitious, she felt almost a sense of destiny regarding the intertwining of her life with her twin's. As long as she could remain in control, she would never go through the hell Hallie had.

Hannah had to clench her teeth to keep from groaning. Her fear was cowardly and irrational and totally unscientific. But it was real.

"Damn, damn, damn. I must be fatally flawed."

She didn't realize she'd spoken aloud until she heard Jim's voice. "Did you say something, Hannah?"

"No. Go back to your typing."

She stared through the skylight, listening to the clatter of typewriter keys and plotting how she would survive the next few days.

•　　•　　•

She'd survive the way she always had—with wit and style.

That was her first thought as she dressed for work the next morning. The first order of the day was to make sure Jim Roman knew exactly who he was dealing with. When she'd finished with him, he'd know that Dr. Hannah Donovan was not a woman to be taken lightly—let alone taken in the kitchen. After this morning there'd be no doubt in his mind that Hannah was a woman best left alone.

She paused at the foot of the stairs and glanced toward Jim's sleeping bag. One arm thrown across his forehead, he had the tousled look of an innocent little boy. Looks were certainly deceiving, she decided.

"Jim," she called his name but not very loudly. "Time to rise and shine." Now she spoke even softer, feeling not the slightest twinge of guilt. After all that business in Greenville—stalking her in her bath, high-handedly taking the stallion away from her, not to mention parading around town in a tablecloth— Jim Roman deserved everything she was going to give him.

A wicked gleam came into her eye as she reached for her tape recorder and turned it on full blast. "Here's to revenge," she said as the whistling, blowing, clicking, and calling of humpback whales filled the room.

"What the hell!" Jim sat straight up in his sleeping bag, a wild look in his eyes. He swung his head around, shaking the last dregs of sleep from his mind, then his gaze fell on Hannah. She was standing with her hands on her hips, laughing.

"What is that godawful racket?"

"My whales," Hannah said innocently. "I thought

since you'd come all this way to do a story about them, you might as well get acquainted right away."

Jim raked his hands through his hair. "Good Lord, what time is it?"

"Five o'clock."

"Five o'clock!"

"I called you, but you didn't wake up."

"Five dammit o'clock." Groaning, he flopped back onto his down bag. "In San Francisco I don't go to bed until nearly five o'clock. Would you mind turning that racket off so I can sleep?"

Hannah turned the volume down, but only a little bit. The song of the humpbacks still resounded through the cabin. "Don't mind me. I'll do my research, and you can sleep. Maybe your story will write itself."

Jim flung back his bag and stood up, as magnificently nude as a Greek statue. "Don't mind me," he called over his shoulder as he paraded by, "I have to start the day with a shower."

Hannah regretted her hasty revenge. Walking to the recorder, she pressed the rewind button. Then she got her pad and a cup of coffee and sat down at her table to work. But it wasn't the song of the humpback she heard: It was the song of Jim Roman in the shower. He was singing some off-color sailor's ditty that probably was calculated to make her squirm. She'd be damned if she'd give him that satisfaction.

When he emerged from the shower, still naked, she looked up, as cool as she could be under the circumstances.

"I leave in fifteen minutes."

"I'll be ready."

It couldn't be soon enough to suit her. Seeing Jim Roman in the buff was enough to turn marble statues to putty. And she was no marble statue. She stomped to her recorder and punched it off.

"Don't forget to wear your coat. It gets cold on the water."

"That's not the only place it gets cold." He fastened his pants and reached for his shirt.

Hannah whirled on him. "What?"

"I said that's not the only place it gets cold. You must have lowered the temperature in this cabin ten degrees."

"*You're* the one who came here. I didn't invite you."

"Damned right I came." He glared at her as he buttoned his shirt up crooked. "It's strictly business."

"Oh, really? If that kiss last night was an example of the way you do business, you must have some very satisfied customers."

Suddenly all the anger drained out of him. "I've been a perfect jackass."

"Not perfect." She gave him a small smile.

"I'm sorry, Hannah." He strode across the room and reached for her.

She stepped back. "Please don't touch me. That's what all this is about."

"I know." He dropped his hands. "I couldn't stay away, Hannah. I had to see you one more time. I guess I had to prove to myself that you were just another woman passing through my life."

"I am, Jim. That's all I can be—for you or any other man." She swept her arms wide, encompassing the cabin and all it stood for. "This is my life. It's harsh and hard, but I love it."

"I know you do," he said softly. Leaning over, he brushed his lips across her cheek. "What do you say we start over?" Tipping back on his heels, he grinned at her. "Good morning, Dr. Donovan."

She smiled. "Good morning, Jim Roman. Are you ready to go to work?"

"Lead the way, Dr. Donovan."

Hannah leaned against the boat railing, the wind ruffling her hair. Her face was alight with excitement as she pointed to Bopeep and gave Jim a running commentary on her work. He checked to make sure his pocket recorder was on, then he went back to what had become his favorite pastime the last few hours—Hannah watching. For the fiftieth time he thought that she was magnificent. She was like one of the wild things that inhabited Glacier Bay, sleek and beautiful and in many ways uncomplicated. Her dedication to her work was total, and her love for the land was astonishing. She got the same pleasure from the jagged cliffs and awesome icebergs of Alaska that he got from the skyscrapers and the Golden Gate bridge of San Francisco.

Worlds apart, he thought, in both location and philosophy. Home to her merely was a place to rest up for her work. Home to him was warm slippers and a glass of wine by the fireside. He thought briefly of his houseboat. Not exactly the house of his dreams, but it would do until the real thing came along—and the right woman.

"Are you listening, Jim?"

He brought his mind to focus on the moment. "To every word. This will be a good story, Hannah. Maybe even one of my best. It makes me wonder if I'm as enchanted with covering the crime scene as I'd always thought."

She gazed at him. "I wonder too."

"What?"

She brushed back a lock of hair the wind had whipped into her face. "Oh . . . nothing." She turned her back on him and faced the water. "As I've told you, whales travel in communities called pods. Each pod has its own unique dialect. The dialect of the humpback evolves from year to year, but those of the other species of whale remain the same."

He crossed over the rail and stood beside her. "You said that mostly males come to the cold arctic waters."

"Yes. The females prefer to stay in warmer waters to calve and raise their families."

"How do they mate?"

She knew he was talking about whales, but the way his voice caressed the words, all silky and seductive, made her think of other things. She looked staunchly out over the water, but no matter how hard she concentrated on whales, she still felt overwhelmed by the solid presence of Jim at her side. "The male goes to the female."

"Yes?" he moved closer, brushing his leg against hers. A slight shiver was the only sign she gave that she'd noticed.

"He returns to warmer waters and searches her out."

"The male whale."

"Yes." She swung her eyes upward to his, and she was caught. "The male searches out the female." The fire in the center of his eyes warmed her. She felt its heat spread through her body. Unconsciously her tongue flicked over her lips.

"All nature's creatures seem to obey that order."

"Yes." The look they exchanged was long and deep. "He goes to her once a year."

"Only once?"

"Only once. He stays for several months, then returns to colder waters."

"And the female conceives?"

"Not always." She couldn't pull away from his gaze. "In fact, the female whale gives birth on the average of only once every ten years."

"Then they must have sex partially for the enjoyment of it."

"What?"

"The whales."

"Oh, the whales."

"Do you think they enjoy sex?"

"I don't know."

"It would make an intriguing study, Doctor."

Although Jim had made no move to touch her, she felt as if he'd stripped her clothes off and laved her body with his tongue. She knew her cheeks must be bright pink from the heat of her passion.

"If you ever do such a study," Jim continued, "I'd be glad to help you."

"On sex?"

"Yes." He backed away from the railing. "Whales. If you ever decide to do an intensive study on the mating habits of whales, let me know. I want to write the story."

"Oh, the story."

"Yes."

The loud slapping sound startled them both. Hannah glanced over the railing in time to see Bopeep's mighty flukes bashing the water. She laughed.

"What's he doing?" Jim hurried back to the rail and leaned over.

"He's playing. In the summertime whales love to cavort and socialize. Bopeep knows me, so he's trying to get my attention. Listen." She hastily lowered the hydrophone into the water as the giant humpback began his mysterious song. "Do you hear that, Jim? That's his social language. I think Bopeep is trying to communicate with me."

"He's probably flirting with you, asking you to head down to warmer waters. I would if I were in his shoes."

"You would?"

"If I were a whale."

Turning away from Hannah, Jim reached into his pocket for his pipe. He had a lot of thinking to do, and most of it had nothing whatsoever to do with his magazine story.

It was very late when they returned to Hannah's cabin.

"You keep an exhausting schedule, Dr. Donovan." Jim hung up their parkas and sprawled into a chair beside the fireplace. "Do you do this every day?"

"In the summertime I do. I have to take advantage of the good weather and the long daylight—and the cooperation of the whales. They return to Glacier Bay in the summer in large numbers."

"And the harsh winters?"

"I spend in the institute, compiling my data and writing papers, or traveling, giving lectures."

"And running the Yukon Quest?"

"Yes."

"That's a grueling race. Why do you do it, Hannah?"

"I enjoy the challenge—and the sense of control. There's something extremely satisfying about knowing that I can pit myself and my dog team against nature and come out a winner."

Jim left his chair beside the fireplace and went into the small cooking alcove. "To show my appreciation for a great day, I'm preparing dinner."

"It was a good day, wasn't it, Jim?"

"Yes, it was a very good day."

"Tomorrow I'll take you to the institute."

He smiled at her as if she'd promised to take him to paradise.

Hannah was a-tingle with excitement when she woke up. For a moment she wondered why an ordinary day should make her feel that way, then she remembered that this was no ordinary day. Jim Roman was downstairs. She could hear him stirring already. As she started down the stairs, she squelched her excitement and reminded herself that he was a risk she didn't dare take.

"Are you decent down there?" she called.

"I try never to be decent, but I am dressed."

Jim was wearing jeans, sweatshirt, sweater, and sneakers. "Don't you have some hiking shoes?"

"I don't need hiking shoes on the streets of San Francisco."

"This is not the streets of San Francisco."

His gaze swept her from head to toe. "How well I know," he said softly.

The cabin was suddenly too small and too hot for

Hannah. And much too dangerous. She grabbed her gun and headed for the door. "Let's go. We can have doughnuts and coffee at the institute."

Jim caught up with her on the front path. "Wait a minute, wildcat," he said as he took her elbow. "Do you want to get a city boy lost?"

With the sun backlighting him, Jim looked as if he'd stepped straight out of her dreams. But the hand on her arm was all too real. She closed her eyes briefly, trying to regain her composure. "Maybe I do," she said. "Maybe it would be best for both of us."

"Hannah."

He leaned forward as if he meant to kiss her. Morning seemed to shine in his face. It was more temptation than she could bear. She jerked her head back and saw his jaw tighten.

"Why in the hell do you always carry that gun?" he asked.

"To protect myself against predators."

He rammed his hands into his pockets. "You're safe with me, Dr. Donovan. The only thing I want form you is a story."

"That's great, because that's all you're going to get."

She whirled away from him and started rapidly up the path. Jim ran after her. His thoughts were as black as his temper. Damned independent woman. The least little threat of a kiss and she had her back up like an alley cat. He could keep his hands off her for two more days. There were other women, and there were certainly more pliant women.

He stopped for breath. Hannah was six yards ahead of him, climbing a cliff as if it were a staircase in the Ritz. She was so vibrant, she made the air around her pulse with excitement. Jim groaned. The next two days loomed before him like the gates of hell.

She looked back over her shoulder. "If the climb is too much for you, you can go back to the cabin. I'll give you a report at the end of the day."

"Nothing is too much for me. Lead on."

Gritting his teeth, he followed her. His feet hurt, his side ached, and his stomach was growling from hunger. But he wouldn't give her the satisfaction of knowing his condition. If her game was to make him turn tail and run, she wouldn't succeed.

After what seemed like hours to Jim, the institute finally came into sight. It was nothing more than a primitive log hut hanging on the edge of the cliff they had climbed. A simple wooden sign over the doorway proclaimed its function.

When Hannah turned toward him, she was beaming. He'd noticed that her work always brought that look to her face—and *only* her work. He felt an urge to cuss and didn't know why. "This is it," she was saying. "This is where much of the real work takes place." She escorted him into a room as compact and as highly organized as his boat. Not an inch of space was wasted. File cabinets lined the north wall, two functional desks and a set of bookshelves took up the south wall, and the space in between was given to telescopes and equipment Jim could only begin to guess at. Dr. Sol Thunderburk, the cetologist, was not at the institute during the summer months, Hannah had told him, so the two of them were alone. Jim was achingly aware of that fact.

"Look." He turned in the direction Hannah was pointing. The bay was spread out beyond the wide bank of west windows as big as eternity and so blue, it made his eyes hurt to look at it. The water looked clearer, cleaner, brighter than it did in San Francisco.

"It's spectacular, Hannah." *But no less spectacular than you*, he thought. Both the woman and the ocean were wild and primitive. And equally as hard to tame. What was worse, he didn't even know why he wanted to.

He gazed at her with naked longing.

Turning form the view, Hannah caught the look in his eyes. *Don't look at me like that*, she wanted to scream. Her hand tightened on her gun, and she made herself walk calmly to the coffeemaker. Survival was all-important to her. He'd be gone in a few days, and her life would once again get back to normal.

"Coffee will be ready in a minute or two." She stowed her gun, picked up the can, and started to measure out coffee. "Damn."

"Did you say something?"

"I spilled coffee."

"I'll help you." He was across the room before she could protest. All her breath seemed to leave her as his hands closed over hers. "Steady hands help. Are we making six or eight cups?" His eyebrow quirked upward in question.

"Eight. It's going to be a long day." She tried to pull her hands away, but he held them fast.

"Do I make you nervous?"

"Why should you?"

"Because you want the same thing I do."

"I've learned to ignore my baser instincts. Perhaps you should too."

He threw back his head and roared with laughter. She didn't think what she'd said was so funny, but at least it served to free her hands. She hurried away from Jim while she could. Lord deliver her from that warrior, she thought. And from her primitive instincts, she added as she swung her gaze back toward him. Never had she met a man who so completely enthralled her. He was ruthless and wicked and unscrupulous and brilliant and witty and funny and enchanting. Not to mention dangerous.

She drew herself up and gave him her haughtiest look, the one Jacob called her Hurricane Hannah look. "Are you here to work, or what?"

"Do I have a choice?"

"No."

"In that case, Dr. Donovan, lead me to the sweatshop."

Eight

Again they were pleasantly surprised that they worked so well together. In spite of the rocky beginning, the day went smoothly once they got their sexual frustration out of their minds. It was almost seven before they left the institute.

"This is crazy," Jim remarked as they stepped out into the light. "How can you stand not knowing night from day?"

"It's one of those things I've gotten accustomed to."

"Like doing without sex?"

"Not that again."

"It will always be that with us."

Instead of replying, Hannah lengthened her stride so that she could get ahead of him. Putting a few feet between them helped, but not much.

The first drop of rain took her by surprise. She'd been so busy sparring with Jim, she had broken one of the cardinal rules of a native Alaskan: Always pay attention to the sky. It was dark and heavy with storm clouds.

The summer storm suddenly let loose with all its fury, drenching her within seconds. Thunder ricocheted off the cliffs.

"Jim!" She whirled quickly, calling his name. The rain was coming down in opaque sheets by now. She barely could see her hand in front of her face, much less Jim. Panic seized her. What if he lost his footing on the unfamiliar path? What if he fell and broke his legs—or worse? "Jim!"

"I'm here." She felt herself being enfolded by his arms. "Don't panic, babe. I'm right here."

She peered up through the driving rain, trying to see his face. All she could make out were his white teeth. He was smiling.

"I didn't panic. I never panic. I just didn't want you to fall off the cliff."

"I didn't know you cared, love," he said lightly.

She cared, she thought. In spite of all reason, she cared, but she never would let him know. Pulling back slightly, she said, "Let's get out of this storm. Follow me."

She led him toward a small cave that was tucked into the jagged side of the cliff. "Duck," she ordered, "and hope we aren't trespassing on a wild creature."

"There can be worse fates, Hannah."

The tension in his voice made her jerk around to look at him. In the dimness of the cave he was gazing at her with unmistakable desire. She was trapped. With the storm rampaging outside, she had nowhere to go. He continued watching her in that predatory way, and she felt her own passion rising. Always it was like this between them, she thought.

One look, one touch, and they were engulfed in a magnificent passion.

She inched away, scooting along the damp cave floor so that his thigh was no longer brushing against hers.

"And what are those fates?" she asked.

"Don't you know?"

His gaze fell hungrily upon her. She was no longer sure whether the furious pounding she heard was the storm outside or the raging of her own blood in her ears.

"There could be grizzly bears in here with us instead of mountain lions. That would be considerably worse."

"Hmmmm,"

"Or wolverines. They are quite vicious." Hannah never rattled on and on the way she was now. She was furious at herself—and at Jim. "Would you please stop?"

"Stop what?"

"You know damn well what."

"Spell it out for me, Doctor."

"You're looking at me as if I'm a banquet and you haven't eaten in a year."

"Is that a scientific observation, Doctor?"

"Yes."

In one swift move he closed the small space between them. Nothing touched except their thighs. But for all the effect that had on Hannah, he might as well have ripped away her clothes.

"You are so right. Thunderstorms bring out the beast in me." Reaching out, he ran his hand gently up the back of her neck, capturing a handful of hair and watching it filter slowly through his fingers.

The sensation of her silky hair against his skin never failed to arouse him. "The hungry beast."

Ever so slowly he circled his arms around her and lowered her to the cave floor. Her eyes were luminous in the darkness.

Dipping his head toward hers, he murmured, "I could drown in you—and I think I will."

"Jim." She made the token protest, even as her arms wrapped around his neck and pulled him closer.

"I've fought it for two days, Hannah."

"It's just the storm. Alaskan storms warp the"—she caught her breath as his lips brushed across her throat—"perspective," she managed to say as his bold tongue plunged into the V neck of her blouse and licked the hollow between her breasts.

He worked one button loose, then another. His breathing became labored as he impatiently nudged aside the restraining bit of lace and freed her taut nipples. The raging storm moved inside the cave as he pressed his hot tongue against her flesh.

Need spiraled through her, and she fought to hang on to her control. Even as she arched toward his questing mouth, she told herself that she could stop this madness at any time.

"I've been wanting to taste you like this since I first saw you," he said. "You're even better than I imagined. Sweet. So sweet." His tongue wet, teased, licked until her nipples ached with readiness. "So good . . . so ripe." As he sucked, one of his legs moved across her hips and pinioned her.

Just a while longer, she thought. She'd know the intense burning pleasure of his mouth just a while longer. Her hips began a small rhythm, and that, too, was pleasure almost too great to bear.

"Hannah!" He stretched on top of her and captured her lips. Their kissing was as frenzied as the storm.

Mouths and legs locked, they rolled over the cave floor.

"You are temptation . . ." she panted, "almost too great to resist."

"Don't . . . resist."

"I must."

Every muscle in his body was rigid with need. Every inch of her flesh yielded to him. Their clothes became an enhancement rather than a barrier. The friction of denim against denim served only to fan the flames that burned them.

"Don"t fight it, Hannah." He reached for the waistband of her jeans. "Let it happen."

"No." She put her hand on his to stop him. "Never."

His mouth took hers with renewed ferocity. Words were forgotten as they tried to derive every bit of fulfillment they could from the contact of their lips. His tongue slipped between her teeth and plundered the hot, sweet treasures of her mouth.

She was no longer battling for control: She was battling for sanity. With his tongue pumping into her mouth and his body pacing hers with a rhythm as old as time, she had long ago fallen over the edge of control.

Why not, she asked herself. Why not give in to her needs? It would be a one-night stand. Then he'd leave. What would be the harm?

"Hannah . . . you're . . . my obsession."

And you are mine, she thought. There was the harm. There was the danger. Once would never be enough for them, for either of them.

She struggled slowly up from her passion-drugged state. Easing her lips out of his reach, she whispered, "The storm's over."

Jim's eyes were almost black as he lifted himself on his elbows and looked down at her. "The storm will never be over for us." He rolled off her and quietly buttoned her blouse. "I'm afraid it's just beginning."

"You're afraid?"

"Yes." He leaned against the damp cave wall and took out his pipe. "We can never belong to each other, Hannah. And I won't settle for anything less." He filled his pipe bowl, then took a long drag. The fragrant smoke filled the cave. "It's more than separate careers, separate states. It's who we are."

Her smile was rueful. "Two stubborn people who won't give an inch."

"Precisely."

"I followed you all the way up here and discovered, not much to my surprise, that you're the same untamed independent wildcat I meet in Greenville. I guess I was old-fashioned enough to believe the cliché that absence makes the heart grow fonder."

"Some hearts aren't meant to grow fond."

He sent a ring of smoke into the air before he responded. "Every heart is meant to grow fond."

"Not this one." She leaned her head against the cave wall and studied him. "I believe you're a romantic, Jim."

"The last of the great ones." He turned his piercing gaze toward her. "But you're no cynic, Hannah. You're a woman waiting for the right man."

"No, I'm not waiting."

"Yes. And when you find him, you won't let anything stand in your way—not differences and not stubbornness."

She closed her eyes and inhaled the fragrant smoke of his pipe. The smell was soothing to her. There in the dark shelter of the cave with the rain quietly nourishing the land, she felt a great need to confess.

"It's more than that, Jim," she said softly. "It's more than our differences and our stubbornness. I'm afraid."

He removed his pipe and studied her. The naked vulnerability of her face shocked him. *For once in you life, Jim Roman*, he cautioned himself, *squelch your smart tongue.*

"I'm listening, Hannah."

"I know this is going to sound crazy—it has to do with my being a twin. There's a strange bond between Hallie and me. When she hurts, I hurt. When she cries, I cry."

From his background research before the wedding, Jim knew something of Hallie's history. Premonition made the back of his neck tingle. "And when she fails, you fail?" Hannah looked at him in astonishment. "You're talking about her first marriage, aren't you?"

"Yes."

"Would it surprise you to know that I'm afraid too?"

"The intrepid warrior?"

"Not so intrepid. Not in matters of the heart. You see, my father left my mother when I was very young, too young to understand. Mother is a wonderful woman. I can only blame him. And yet he's my father. What kind of man leaves his wife in poverty?

What flaws did Brick Roman have? And am I like him?"

Hannah reached for his hand. "I'm so sorry, Jim."

"It was a long time ago."

"I think you can never be like him."

"That's reassuring, Doctor." He tried to sound nonchalant, but nevertheless he held on to her hand. Touch was a powerful comfort. He'd sensed this compassion in Hannah, but he'd never known it firsthand. In spite of her stubbornness and independence, Hannah was a fine woman.

Hannah smiled at him. "We're not half bad together when we try, are we?"

"Not half bad," he agreed.

Jim began to hope that when he fell in love, the woman would turn out to be somebody almost exactly like Hannah.

And Hannah began to hope.

They held hands all the way back to the cabin.

Almost self-consciously, Hannah let go. "I—" She stopped talking and looked around the small cabin. Being there with him was too intimate, especially after the shared passion and the shared confidences of the cave. "I haven't run my dogs since you came. I think I'll take them out."

Jim knew what she was doing. "It's probably best. I have to wrap up this story, and you would prove a powerful distraction."

"If you're working when I get back, I'll just tiptoe up the stairs and try not to bother you."

"Great."

He stared at the door for three minutes after she'd

gone. He'd come back to the fire and been burned again, he thought. But this time it was different. He was leaving with a heart burdened not only with unfulfilled passion but with knowledge. Hannah was afraid and vulnerable. He never would take advantage of that. If she hadn't confessed . . . if *he* hadn't confessed . . . Angrily he cast those thoughts aside. His best course of action was to finish his story and get out, put the whole episode behind him, chalk it up as experience.

He set up his typewriter and rolled in a sheet of paper. For a while the blankness was his enemy. Then slowly his brain switched into overdrive, and he settled back for the ride. His last conscious thought was that someday things might change for them.

He was hardly aware of her coming in and slipping up the stairs.

Jim woke up before Hannah.

There was an eerie quiet in the cabin, a stillness that was peculiar to the predawn hours. He lay perfectly still in his sleeping bag. Above him, in the loft, Hannah turned on her bed and moaned softly in her sleep. The sound drove a small wedge into Jim's heart.

His story was finished. There was no longer any reason for him to stay in Glacier Bay. He rose quietly from his sleeping bag and stood gazing upward. Every inch of his flesh yearned for Hannah.

Quietly he escaped out the door. Pete rose from his lookout on the front porch and trotted over to him. He was even going to miss her dog, he thought as he leaned down to scratch behind Pete's ears. *Go,* the voice of reason said to him. *Go now before it's too late.* Too late for what he could only imagine. Too late before they hurt each other the way his father had hurt his mother? Too late before they discovered that they'd compromised their careers for the sake of passion? Too late before he felt smothered in a wilderness that barely had running water?

He didn't know. All he knew was that the time had come for him to leave. And he'd do it without fanfare. It would be less painful that way—for both of them.

The dog followed him down the front steps and stood alertly by as Jim did something he hadn't done since he was seven years old: He picked a bouquet of flowers.

Hannah was still asleep when he climbed the stairs to her loft. She was curled on her side with her cheek cuddled into her right palm. In the blush of dawn she looked as dewy and fresh as the maiden flowers in his hand.

He leaned down and carefully placed the white flowers on her pillow. A drop of dew fell from the petals onto her cheek. It glistened there like a single bright tear. He held his breath as her eyelashes fluttered. He didn't want her to see him there. When Hannah awakened, he wanted her to see nothing except the tiny white flowers, their petals shining with dew.

She gave a soft sigh and settled back into her dreams. Her lips curved into a tender smile. Jim tiptoed back down the stairs and quietly began to pack.

• • •

When Hannah awakened, the first thing she realized was that she'd slept later than usual. She started to fling back the covers when she felt the damp softness near her hand. The bouquet of white maiden flowers lay beside her.

Smiling, she lifted them to her face, feeling the dew and inhaling the perfume. She swung her feet off the side of her bed and called softly, "Jim?"

There was no answer. It wasn't like him to be up and about so early, she thought. For the past four days she'd always been the first up, always been the one to awaken him. She sat very quietly, listening for the sounds of the shower. There were none.

"Jim?" She called louder this time, but her only answer was silence.

A small fear turned into a full-fledged case of panic. The flowers fluttered to her pillow as she grabbed her robe and plunged down the stairs. His bedroll was gone, his typewriter was gone, his bag was gone.

When she burst through her front door, she didn't know whether to laugh or to cry. Jim was leaning against a post, looking out over the bay, smoking his pipe. He turned at the sound of her footsteps.

"Did you get my flowers?"

She put her hand over her heart to still its panicked beating. "I thought you had gone."

"I thought about it. When I placed the flowers on your pillow, I meant to let that be my farewell." He tamped out his pipe and stuck it into his pocket. "I don't like good-byes."

"No. I remember. You don't." She clutched her bathrobe around her neck to give her hands something to do. Jim was leaving, she thought. He had meant to leave as casually as he had in Greenville. She'd survived another invasion of the West Coast Warrior. Or had she? Her mind swung back to the cave, then to the tiny bouquet of maiden flowers on her pillow.

"But when I saw you there"—he took one step toward her, then stopped—"so beautiful and innocent-looking." He advanced another step, then another, and finally he was approaching her with a purpose. "I knew I could never leave you."

He swept her against his chest and tipped her face upward.

"Never?" she whispered.

"Not without saying good-bye."

His lips took hers savagely, as if he could deny the good-bye with the fierceness of his kiss. She matched his passion with a fire of her own. For three days she'd worked beside this man, denying herself the pleasures of loving him, concentrating all her energies on helping him get a superb story. And now he was leaving, and there was no longer any need for pretense.

In the early morning stillness they clung together as if they meant never to let go. There was no sound except their hungry murmurings and the thumping of Pete's tail against the wooden porch.

Suddenly, in the distance, they heard the unmistakable chugging of a motor. Jim lifted his head.

"Sleddog's coming."

"Here?"

"Yes. When he brought me to your cabin, I asked him to come by today to pick me up."

"I would have taken you into Gustavus. My van is at the bottom of the cliff."

He cupped her face. "I know, but I hate having to say good-bye at the airport."

The sound of the motor grew louder. "He's almost here." Hannah fought for control as Jim's fingers caressed her cheeks. He leaned down, almost as if he would kiss her again, then he straightened back up and looked off into the distance.

"Hannah . . ."

"Yes?"

His gaze swung back to her. "You . . . belong here. Your work is wonderful."

"So is yours."

The honking of a horn announced the arrival of Sleddog's pickup truck at the foot of the cliff below Hannah's cabin. Jim released her and picked up his gear. "You have a standing invitation to come see me . . . any Thursday."

With a final salute he walked swiftly away, down her path, and down the rocky cliffside. Then the old truck headed back into civilization, bearing away the West Coast Warrior.

Nine

The sun penetrated the mists of San Francisco and shone down on Jim Roman's boat. He was stripped to the waist, stretched in the sunshine, watching Colter Gray Wolf repair his inboard engine.

"What's the problem this time, Colter?"

Dr. Colter Gray Wolf glanced up from his work. Although he was flat on his stomach, leaning over the hull where the engine was housed, not a speck of grease marred him. He had the lean, clean, chiseled look of a museum bronze.

"Spark plugs." He grinned. "I expect my usual fee for doing your repair work."

"Sorry to disappoint you."

"No steaks? I should leave you to flounder on your own."

"How does halibut sound? It's marinating right now in a special concoction of herbs and spices."

Colter made a final adjustment to the engine, then pulled the cover back over the housing. His expression was inscrutable as he cleaned his hands and sat down on the mahogany deck, ankles crossed in the manner of the Apache Indian.

"Tell me about the woman."

Jim had long since grown accustomed to Colter's uncanny ability to read his mind. Although he'd never said anything to his friend beyond the fact that he'd met Hannah in Greenville and was going to Alaska to do a story on her work, it seemed that Colter had tapped into the secret places of his mind.

"What tipped you off, the halibut?"

"Your heart. You've been wearing it on your sleeve."

"That bad, huh?"

"Yes. There's nothing stoic about you, my friend. When I met you at the airport yesterday, I saw that you'd found more in Alaska than a story."

"It's Hannah." Colter nodded and sat waiting patiently for Jim to continue. "She's independent and outspoken and stubborn. And she's about as easy to live with as a box full of wildcats."

"You love her."

"What?" Jim jerked his head up as if he'd been slapped. "That's impossible. She bears about as much resemblance to my dream girl as a panther does to a pussycat."

"Ahh, yes. The dream girl."

"A man has to have visions."

"True. The trick is knowing the difference between a vision and a rationalization." It was Jim's turn to wait. His mind was leaping ahead, anticipating Colter's line of reasoning, but he waited for his friend to elaborate. "A vision leads us forward; a rationalization holds us back."

"You're saying I've used the vision of my dream girl all these years to hold me back?"

"In essence, yes. The shock of having someone you love desert you can sometimes be felt for a lifetime."

Jim didn't have to ask to know Colter was talking about Brick Roman. They'd often shared stories of their childhood; Jim's stories inevitably had led to Brick—big and brash and full of life—the man who had sailed off on *The Black Rover*.

"Your mother has been the only constant in your life, and she's the epitome of a sweet, old-fashioned woman. It's only natural that you've told yourself for years you wanted a woman exactly like her. And yet your father has been the biggest influence in shaping your life. I think you're scared to death of finding a woman like him—someone independent and outspoken and stubborn, someone who will sail out of your life."

"Psychology 101, Dr. Gray Wolf?"

"Indian wisdom, West Coast Warrior. Take it for whatever it's worth."

"I think it's worth a bottle of California's finest." Jim rose from the deck and lifted a bottle of wine out of the cooler. "Gallo." He grinned. "What do you say we go on a binge and forget all about women?"

"Hand me the firewater."

When he saw her picture in the paper three days later, Jim knew he never could forget about women, or rather, one woman, Hannah Donovan. "'World-renowned marine biologist," the paper said, "Dr. Hannah Donovan, will be lecturing at the Leviathan Foundation. . . ." Jim's heart did a quick rhumba against his ribs. She was coming to San Francisco, he thought wildly. Hannah would be *there*, in his city, in . . . He quickly scanned the paper for the date. Eight days. Hannah would be there in eight days.

They were the longest eight days of Jim's life. During that time he changed his mind a dozen times. At first, he definitely would go, then he definitely would not. He didn't sleep, he didn't eat, he lost weight. But most of all, he searched his soul. The conclusion he came to startled him: Hannah was his dream woman. All the while he'd thought he was searching for a sweet, old-fashioned homemaker, he'd been looking for someone exactly like Hannah, a woman with fire and spirit, a woman who would be just as exciting fifty years in the future as she had been the day he met her.

He was so thrilled by his revelation that he got up out of bed, climbed up to his deck, and shouted his happiness to the stars.

Colter's quiet voice drifted from the boat beside his. "Unless my ears are deceiving me, I'm hearing an Indian love call."

Jim went to the boat's railing and leaned across. "Colter? Did I wake you? What are you doing up this time of night?"

"Communing with nature and watching over you, my friend." As his eyes adjusted to the darkness, Jim could make out Colter, leaning against the railing of his boat. "I've felt your agony the last few days, so I've kept a sleeping pallet on deck. Do you need to talk?"

"It's settled. I love her."

"I knew you did. So, what are your plans?"

In the still of the night their quiet voices drifted across the water. Jim had an eerie sense that sometimes love demanded the reverence of hushed voices.

"She's coming here. I'll go to her . . . then I'll wait."

"That's wise. A woman should give some sign."

"I won't keep you any longer. Surgeons need their sleep. Good night, Colter."

Jim leaned farther across the rail to get a better look at his good friend, but Colter already had blended in with the darkness.

The air conditioner in the auditorium wasn't working.

Hannah sat on the small raised platform, sweating and looking out across the audience. Most of San Francisco's intellectuals had turned out, but there was no sight of an auburn-haired giant of a man. The West Coast Warrior wasn't coming.

She wiped a trickle of perspiration off the side of her face and tried not to be disappointed. She never should have come, she told herself. She didn't like to admit to herself why she had come. Ordinarily she turned down all summer lecture invitations. But after Jim had left Glacier Bay, she had come across one lying on her desk. In a moment of madness she had called to see if the foundation still wanted her. They had.

And so, she thought, here she was, against all scientific reason, looking for the man she'd sparred with and spurned, searching the audience for the

West Coast Warrior when she should be thinking of humpback whales.

Vaguely she heard her name being announced, heard the applause. She gathered her scattered wits and rose to talk about the thing she loved most—her work. The lights were lowered because she used slides to accompany her speech, and she proceeded to hold her audience captive—she hoped—for forty-five minutes.

"Dr. Donovan will take questions," the moderator announced after her lecture.

The lights came up just as the man in the back of the room rose from his chair.

"Let's talk about mating, Dr. Donovan—" The speaker paused to let the ripple of laughter die down.

From the first word he'd spoken, Hannah had felt a thrill start in her toes and spread throughout her body. It was an earth-shattering experience, somewhat like an iceberg splintering off the face of a glacier. Her gaze skimmed across the heads of her audience until it rested on Jim, who stood far in the back, looking slimmer than she remembered but every bit as delicious.

"Of whales," he clarified when the laughter ceased.

"Yes?" She barely could speak around the lump in her throat.

"Does the male always seek out the female?"

"Always."

The moderator leaned across the platform. "Could you speak a little louder, Dr. Donovan? I'm afraid the audience didn't catch the answer to that question."

Hannah cleared her throat and spoke directly into the microphone. "Always."

"You're speaking strictly of whales, Dr. Donovan?"

Even across the room she could feel Jim's relentless gaze probing into her, seeing things that no other man had ever seen.

"Yes. Although the male pursuit of the female is a fairly common practice among other mammals."

"Man, for instance?"

"Yes. However, modern times have altered that pattern. Sometimes the female pursues the male."

Jim smiled. "That's all I wanted to know, Dr. Donovan."

Jim felt ten feet tall when he sat down. He had his answer now. Hannah had come to him. He watched as she fielded questions. She was glorious, brilliant. He might have sat there for five minutes or five years. When she was near, time meant nothing to him. There was only the moment, and Hannah, bright as a flame.

He sat through the questions, the rustling and milling of the crowd breaking up. And suddenly Hannah was there, standing beside him, those star-sapphire eyes so bright, they nearly blinded him.

He held out his hand. "You came."

"Yes." Without hesitation she put her hand in his.

"You're not booked into a hotel." It was a statement more than a question.

"No."

He squeezed her hand. "Where are your things?"

She nodded in the direction of a small office.

"Have you had dinner yet?"

"No."

He took her to the Fairmount Hotel on Nob Hill.

"I come to this restaurant only on very special occasions," he explained after they had been seated. "This is the second time I've come."

"Thank you," she said simply. She thought that being one of Jim Roman's special occasions was one of the best things that had ever happened to her. "What was the first occasion?"

"In celebration of my first job as a reporter. I brought my mother."

Hannah leaned forward, her attention riveted by his disclosure. Jim had never talked of his family. "It's very elegant. She must have loved it."

Jim's smile was bittersweet. "She did, but she was scared to death."

"Why?"

"She was afraid her dress wasn't fancy enough and that she'd forgotten all the fine manners of her upbringing. She worried the whole evening."

"She sounds very dear."

"She is. But enough about the past." Jim reached across the table and took her hand. "I've thought of you—more often than I care to mention."

"And I've thought of you."

"What did you think, Hannah?"

"I thought about the fireworks that are always between us." She waited for the waiter to serve their soup. "And I thought that I had been a fool."

He pushed his soup aside so that he could lean closer to her across the table. In the candlelight she was the most achingly gorgeous woman he had ever seen. Seeing her again confirmed what he had told Colter Gray wolf—that he was in love with Dr. Hannah Donovan. "Make that two of us, beautiful woman."

He lifted her hand and pressed his tongue into the middle of her palm. Her eyes widened and her pulse gently vibrated in the hollow of her throat. Neither of them spoke for a long while.

The waiter came with their salads. "Sir?" his nod indicated the untouched soup.

"We've finished," Jim told him.

"It's scrumptious," Hannah murmured.

"Delicious," Jim agreed.

The waiter had been well trained in discretion and politeness. Only his twitching lips betrayed his amusement as he took their untouched soup away.

"Incredible," Jim said as his tongue moved to the pulse spot on Hannah's wrist. "And I'm so hungry."

"For halibut?"

"For you."

"And I for you." Now that she had said it, Hannah finally admitted the truth to herself. By coming to San Francisco she'd merely followed her feelings. For the second time in her life she was putting aside her career to follow the dictates of her heart. "Do you think this special occasion might be postponed for a little scientific research?"

"On what subject, Doctor?"

"Mating habits."

"Whales?" His smile told her he was teasing.

"Of female scientists and male reporters."

The breathless promise in her voice almost undid him. It was a moment before he could get his passion under control enough to reply, and still longer before he could stand. "Wait right here," he told her as he went in search of their waiter. It took him only five minutes to settle their bill and come back to the table for her.

They caught a taxi outside the Fairmount.

Jim waved a large bill into the driver's hand. "This is for you if you can get us to the waterfront in fifteen minutes flat."

The cabdriver grinned. "No problem, buddy."

They sat side by side on the backseat, not speaking as the cab hurtled through the night. Hannah cast her eyes sideways at Jim. He was as implacable as the ice-draped St. Elias Mountain that guarded her cabin. Even the hand that held hers told her nothing. There would be no promises, she told herself, no talk of the future between them. She was seizing the moment in much the same way she had with Rai. And Lord help her make it work this time, she prayed.

She smelled the ocean before she saw his houseboat. It rose out of the water, small and neat and compact, an aging yacht of polished mahogany and gleaming white paint.

The taxi pulled to a stop, and the driver bowed majestically as he opened the door. "I hope everything works out to your satisfaction, mate." He was grinning when he revved the engine and roared down the cobblestone street.

Jim took both Hannah's hands and turned her so that they were facing. "I'm glad you sought me in warm waters, Hannah."

"This is not commitment, Jim."

"I know."

The fire in his eyes almost consumed her. "Nor love."

"No." He moved so close, their breath mingled in the warm summer night. Releasing one hand, he cupped the back of her neck and lifted her hair. The moon gave it the glow of black diamonds.

He let her satin hair fall, then he scooped her into his arms and carried her aboard his boat. The familiar gentle rocking motion under his feet reassured him. Ducking his head, he carried her below deck. The moonlight, pouring through the portholes, lit his way.

Hannah sighed as he lowered her to the bed. "I've been waiting for this for a long, long time," she whispered.

"I'll make it worth the wait."

She didn't know what she had missed most, she thought, that beguiling arrogance or the wicked way he cocked his eyebrow upward.

"Is that a promise?"

He hauled her against him, fitting the entire length of her body into his. Through all their clothes she could feel his arousal. "What do you think?" he asked.

Her hands dragged his shirt loose from his pants and skimmed over his smooth back. "Don't tell me; show me."

At her touch, desire exploded in him. It took all his willpower not to tear off their clothes and take her immediately in a wild, mindless frenzy. Clamping an iron control on his passion, he slowly unbuttoned her jacket and her blouse. To his delight, Hannah was wearing the most feminine of all garments under her business suit—a pink silk teddy. His hands skimmed over the silky garment, arousing her nipples to hard peaks. With his thumb he unsnapped the waistband of her skirt, then he flattened his hand and slid it, palm down, over her stomach. He thought the combination of silk against well-toned muscles to be the most erotic in the world.

His hand delved lower until he was cupping her soft, warm mound. She sucked her breath in.

"Do you like that, Hannah?"

"Hmmmm." She leaned into him, and her tongue found the pulse spot at the base of his throat. "Hmmmm," she murmured as his fingers pushed aside silk and slipped into her welcoming warmth.

She rocked against him as her tongue played over his throat.

"Ahh, Hannah. Hannah."

He unzipped her skirt and slid it down her legs. They were as perfect as he'd remembered, long and slim and finely muscled. Propping himself on his elbows, he gazed down at her, drinking in his fill. She looked just the way he'd imagined—her face love-flushed, her dark hair tumbled across the pillows. He lifted a strand of her hair to his lips.

"You're a beautiful wildcat. Just looking at you is the most powerful aphrodisiac in the world."

She arched upward and wrapped her arms around his chest. "How powerful?"

"This." Swiftly he bent down and with his tongue wet the silk over her left breast. Lifting his head, he gazed down at his handiwork. Her nipple pushed against the silk, dark rose and delectable. "And this," he said as he lowered his mouth over the jutting nipple. He sucked, reveling in the sensation of wet silk on his mouth and the readiness of Hannah's body. "And this . . ." His mouth traveled across to her other breast.

She arched against him. "Please, please." Shrugging one shoulder, she worked the right strap of her teddy down. Jim's mouth nudged the silk lower until her breast was exposed.

He sucked his breath in as the creamy mound came into view. "Perfection . . ." His mouth closed over her. "Ummmm, heavenly." He teased the nipple with his tongue, then, unable to resist any longer, he took her deep into his mouth. She moaned as he sucked.

And soon it wasn't enough—for either of them. Lifting himself on one elbow, he skimmed the pink silk slowly downward. His eyes glowed with love as inch by inch her body came into view.

Lowering his head, he licked his tongue over the soft down of her stomach. "I have to have you . . . all of you."

Hannah tangled her hands in his hair and gave herself up to wild, wanton passion that was controlling her. Who could fight destiny, she wondered.

She rode the waves of desire that swept over her. "Jim . . . ahhh, yes . . . Jim." His name was a sigh on her lips.

She seemed to be floating against the pillows as he rose above her, magnificent as any warrior of ancient Rome. The eerie half light from the moon lent his wide chest a glow of magic as he stripped off his clothes. Then he was over her, covering her with every inch of that body she'd wanted since her sister's wedding in Greenville. Her fingernails dug into his back as she tried to hold on to the last shreds of her control. This was mere lust, she told herself. As Jim pumped into her, she sensed his own struggle for control.

The timeless, ancient rhythms of love became a battle as each fought to hang on to separate dreams. They rolled, locked together, taking what they'd wanted since they first met.

Just this once, Hannah thought. *Then I'll put him behind me.*

One time, Jim told himself, *then she'll be out of my system.*

As the wonder of their joining sang through them, both lowered their shields and gave up the battle. It was a subtle shifting, and neither knew when it had happened. They knew only when it was over that some miracle had taken place, a breathless magic that was completely beyond their control.

Jim lifted himself on his elbows and looked down at Hannah. Raising a strand of her tangled hair to his lips, he said, "A man could get addicted to you."

Hannah reached up and traced his scar. "A woman could become used to having you around."

Neon lights and skyscrapers and big city crime paled beside the reality of Hannah. And Jim knew that, in spite of his many avowals of what he wanted in a woman, he was in love with Hannah Donovan. He actually groaned. Lord, if there was ever a mismatch, it was the two of them.

"Hannah . . ."

"Shhh . . . don't talk, Jim," She reached for him.

And they were lost once more in the magic of the moment.

Hannah woke up smiling. "Jim." She reached across the covers and touched empty space.

"So, the sleeping beauty is finally up." Jim stood in the galley, wrapped in a big apron and wreathed in an even bigger smile.

"Oh, my gosh. What time is it?" She started to swing her legs off the bed, but Jim crossed the small space and put them back.

"We have hours before your plane leaves."

•

"How do you know?"

"Your plane tickets were in your jacket pocket." His apron hit the carpet with a soft thump.

"You looked?" Smiling, Hannah reached for his belt buckle.

"A good investigative reporter never lets scruples overcome sense." His shirt fell into the heap of clothes. He buried his face in her neck. "Mmmm, you smell better than a morning cup of coffee."

"They say the proof is in the tasting."

"I'm dying to find out."

Much later, they went up on deck for breakfast.

"I planned to serve breakfast long ago. I hope you like cold omelets, Hannah." Jim reached down to help her up the ladder.

"My favorite kind." She gasped as she stepped on deck. There was nothing as far as the eye could see except water. "What happened to San Francisco?"

"Sometime in the night I left it behind." He pulled out a canvas chair and seated her at his small table. "I wanted an appropriate setting."

"For breakfast?"

"No. For a proposal. Will you marry me, Hannah?"

Her fork clanked onto her plate. Without any warning, without any fanfare, Jim Roman had proposed. As casually as he'd walked into her life, he'd asked her to become his wife, right between the coffee and the eggs.

"You're joking, of course." Hannah put her hands in her lap to control their shaking.

"I would never joke about anything as serious as

marriage. I'm asking you to share my life, Hannah. Will you?"

He hadn't said a word about love. Her mind spun backward to the night and the bed they'd shared. Every touch, every caress, had spoken love. She didn't need words to know that Jim Roman was in love with her—and she with him. The sudden knowledge stunned her. All the while she'd sparred with him, run from him, run *to* him, she had been fooling herself. She was deeply in love with the man sitting across the table from her.

"Hell, I'm not what you would call a good catch," he said into the silence. "I'm just a simple reporter who suddenly has found himself in a predicament. I didn't mean to fall in love with you, Hannah, but I did it anyway. It just seemed to happen, and when it did, I took the next logical step. When you're certain, why wait?"

"I love you too."

He was so busy planning his next step he almost missed what she'd said. "What did you say?"

"I said I love you, Jim Roman, and I think you're a very romantic man."

His excitement propelled him from the chair. "I'll call a preacher. I'll call Mom."

"Jim . . ."

"I'll call Colter."

"Jim . . ."

"Hell, I'll even call the National Guard."

Hannah left her chair and hugged her arms around his chest. She buried her face against him so that her voice was muffled by his shirt. "I can't marry you, Jim."

"What did you say?" he pulled her back and tipped

her face up with one finger. "Hannah. What did you say?"

"No," she said softly. "The answer is no."

"We won't always live on a houseboat. I'm planning to build a little cottage."

Her heart almost broke at the eagerness on his face. "And have children?"

"Yes. Lots of them. I never had brothers and sisters. I think a big family would be great."

"And live happily ever after?" Each word he said was a big stone in her heart.

"I think that's the general idea."

"You're forgetting my career, Jim."

"Hell, Hannah. I don't care if you want to watch whales. You can give lectures. You can do whatever your heart desires."

"You make my career sound like a hobby. It's not!"

It was a while before he spoke, and when he did, his voice was quiet. "I won't stand in the way of your career."

"My work is in Alaska."

The expression on his face became fierce. The previous night when he'd planned this proposal, it had never occurred to him that she might say no. Her body already had said it all. She loved him. She'd even said so herself. To him it was simple. Love meant marriage. Dammit, he *wanted* it to be that simple. "We can work that out."

"How? Are you going to move to Glacier Bay?"

He swung his head around and gazed across the Pacific. The waters looked calm and peaceful and so blue, a man could almost believe he was looking straight into heaven. Behind him was the city he loved and beside him was the woman he loved.

"We'll make it work."

"No, Jim. I won't ask you to leave your work behind, and I won't leave mine. I risked my career once. I won't do it again."

"Did you love him?"

She turned her face away and gazed into the distance. Jim cupped her chin and turned her back around.

"Dammit, did you love him?"

"I—" His compelling gaze demanded the truth. "I don't know, Jim. It was lust, affection; it might even have been love."

"It wasn't."

"How do you know? You can't know that."

"If it had been true love, you would have worked things out. Hannah." His hands gripped her face as she tried to turn away again. "Dammit, wildcat. Look at me. You didn't *love* him. You love me. It makes all the difference in the world."

"None. It makes none."

"You're stubborn."

"So are you—a stubborn romantic."

They glared at each other. Then they were in each other's arms, kissing as if the world would end before they got enough.

Jim groaned. "Don't do this to us."

"I'm not . . . I can't . . . oh, Jim. Just love me. Please, just love me."

With nothing surrounding them except the blue waters and the tranquility of the morning, Jim lowered Hannah to the deck and loved her.

And when it was over, she left him.

Bidding him not to come, she went below and quietly dressed. She was doing the right thing, she told herself, the *only* thing. There could be no compromise between the two of them—the wildcat, as he had dubbed her, and the West Coast Warrior. Each of them belonged in a separate world, and never the twain would meet.

Her footsteps sounded like the voice of doom as she climbed up to where he was waiting.

"Take me back."

"There's still time—"

"Please. I want to go back now."

"Tempting as it might be, I don't plan to shanghai you." His face was grim as he turned the boat toward San Francisco.

Ten

Hannah had insisted on coming to the airport alone, and now she was glad she had. She didn't want Jim to see her cry. Being right shouldn't hurt so much, she thought.

Once she was back in Glacier Bay, she immersed herself in her work. To her surprise, she found that the primal longing of her body didn't interfere with her work; rather, it gave her a sharp edge of awareness she hadn't had before. She seemed to see old problems with a clearer perspective; she seemed to find answers that had eluded her.

The days passed with no word from Jim, and she came to beleive he had accepted her decision. From time to time she looked up at the imagined sound of footsteps on her front porch. He'd come back, she'd think, and half start from her chair. But it would only be Pete, moving around to get a better sleeping position.

She'd been wise; she'd been sensible. And she'd been very, very foolish. As the empty days passed,

she realized that she should have countered his offer of marriage with the offer of an affair. They
could have flown to see each other on occasion. But
she'd closed the door to everything. She'd said no
while her body had been screaming yes.

She almost rose from bed and went to the telephone. Then another thought struck her. If she
made her offer, Jim would be insulted—and hurt. A
man with marriage on his mind would never settle
for an affair. Why did she think he had been silent
since she'd left San Francisco? He'd offered himself
to her, and she'd turned him down.

It was over. All of it.

As she lay in bed, staring at the strange half light
of summer that filtered in through her skylight, she
mourned her loss.

She was distracted the next day. Bopeep didn't
show, and the few whales that did cavorted only
briefly around her research vessel before sounding.
By noon she was feeling so cantankerous that she
was glad nobody was around to see her. Her irrita-
tion was heightened by the approaching speedboat.
Didn't that fool know she was trying to work? Whoever he was, he was scaring away all the whales.

As the boat pulled alongside, she leaned over to
yell her frustration. The red-haired man at the helm
gave her a bright salute.

"Jacob!" Thinking she'd been tricked by the glare
on the water, she shaded her eyes. "Jacob? Is that
you?"

"Yes. Heave to, Hannah, so I can come aboard."

"Where in the world did you come from?" she

asked after he had secured his small boat and boarded her vessel. Holding his face between her hands, she rained kisses on his face. "Why didn't you let me know you were coming? Oh, Lord, Jacob, I'm so glad to see you, I could cry."

"Hey, sis . . . hey." Jacob pulled her into a teddy bear hug. "You *are* crying. Tell big brother all about it."

Hannah made a valiant effort to hide her tears. "Big, my eye. You'll always be the baby in the Donovan family—besides being the runt."

"Runt!" Jacob roared. "I'll show you runt!" He picked her up and waltzed around the deck, holding her feet six inches off the floor. "Waaaltz-zzing Maatiil-daaa, waaalt-ziiing Matil-daaaa," he sang.

"Put me down, you crazy man."

"Not until you laugh." He continued his crazy waltz and off-key singing, his blue eyes twinkling like twin comets in his sunbronzed face. "Come on, Hannah. Laugh. Thaaat's a girl."

He set her back on her feet. "Now, tell me who has made you cry so I can beat the hell out of him."

"It's nothing. It's me. . . ." She pushed her heavy hair back from her face. "I don't want to talk about it right now. I want to talk about you. Where have you been this time?"

Jacob gave her one last assessing look, then assumed his eternal devil-may-care posture. "In South America. They had an oil-field fire that outdid the one in Saudi last Christmas."

"Jacob." Hannah reached for his face again. "I worry about you. Your work is so dangerous."

He grinned. "Nothing can happen to me. I'm the

best damned trouble-shooting firefighter in the world."

She laughed. "If self-confidence counts, you are. Have you eaten? You look kind of gaunt."

"I lost my appetite in Seattle."

Hannah's head snapped up. "You've been to Seattle?"

"Yes. I headed straight there after I left South America. My Learjet's still there. I bummed around the city a few days, then decided to rent a Cessna and head on up to see you."

"Did you see Rachel?"

Jacob turned away from her and gazed out over the water. She saw the pain that flitted briefly across his face.

"No. I didn't go to see Rachel. I went to visit the city."

She thought he might be covering up, but she couldn't tell. With Jacob she was never sure of anything except his love for his family and his love for flight. Since he was three years old, he'd been fascinated with anything that could get off the ground. He'd suffered more broken bones than any of his brothers or sisters because he'd always been trying to rig a set of wings or a flying machine for himself—and he'd been intrepid about trying out all his inventions.

Hannah decided not to press about Rachel. After all, she didn't want to talk about Jim. She and Jacob were alike in that respect: They liked to keep their counsel.

"Come inside." She took his hand and led him toward the galley. "I'll fix us a sandwich, and you can tell me about Seattle."

They talked until midnight. Then they headed toward shore. After they had docked and walked to Hannah's cabin, they prepared a salmon for dinner and continued their marathon of talking.

At three A.M. Jacob popped some corn.

"Just to keep us awake," he said.

"It's because you're a bottomless pit. I don't know how you can eat so much and still keep from having a pot belly."

"I'm saving my pot belly for later. It's one of the decadent pleasures I plan to enjoy in my old age." He added lots of salt and plenty of butter to the popcorn, just the way he knew his sister liked it. "Actually," he said as he placed the bowl of popcorn on the table between them, "I'm hoping to soften you up and wear you down so you'll come clean with me."

She delved into the popcorn and stuffed a generous handful into her mouth. "What do you mean, come clean?" she asked after she'd swallowed.

"For a woman with a Ph.D., you can be mighty dense. Don't you get lonesome up here in this wilderness, Hannah? Don't you ever need a shoulder to cry on?"

"Not often enough to change my ways." She reached for more popcorn. "Of course, I usually talk to Hallie on the phone, but I'll be damned if I'll be the one to throw a wet blanket over her honeymoon."

"She's still on a honeymoon? Where in the devil are they?"

Hannah chuckled. "Back in Florence, Alabama. They've been back for weeks now. I'll show you the card." She got up and rummaged in her desk drawer until she came up with the bright postcard. "We're back home," it said. "What a wonderful, marvelous, fabulous marriage we're having."

Jacob laughed. "That sounds just like Hallie."

"See what I mean. She'll always be on her honeymoon."

Jacob laid the card on the table and looked at his sister. "Throw that wet blanket on me. I'm sure as hell not having a fabulous marriage—and I don't plan to."

"Neither do I."

"You say that as if you've been giving it some thought."

"I have—lately. Since I met Jim Roman."

"Ahh, that big man who came down to cover Hallie's wedding. I liked him."

"I did too. But I have no plans to mess up his life—or mine— with marriage."

"I applaud your wisdom, sis. But I'm not so sure you'd mess up."

"Hallie did her first time around. And look how long it took Tanner and Amanda to get it right. Eleven years."

"But look at them now. Boy, if I thought—" Jacob abruptly cut off what he'd been about to say. He reached over and wiped a smear of butter off Hannah's chin. "I'm not qualified to give advice on anybody's love life, but I do know this: You're the smartest, most determined woman I know, and if you decide to give marriage a try, I believe you can make it work."

"Thanks, Jacob."

"You're welcome," he said around a huge yawn. "I think I'll hit the sack, Hannah. You've talked me out."

"I've talked *you* out. I ought to make you take your sleeping bag out to the kennels."

Jacob got up from the table and went to his bedroll, singing "Hard-hearted Hannah" in his flat baritone. The last thing he heard before his head hit the pillow was the sound of Hannah's laughter.

Jacob stayed three days. They were glorious, laughter-filled days, days when Hannah thought of nothing more pressing than how to beat him at poker.

But when he was gone, he took the brightness with him. Even a long training run with her sled dogs didn't lift Hannah's spirits. When she went to bed that night, she vowed that tomorrow would be a new day.

She'd put Jim Roman out of her life once and for all. She didn't know how she would do it, but she was Dr. Hannah Donovan, educated and independent. She'd find a way.

Hannah was alert the instant she heard Pete growl. She reached for her .300 Magnum and her robe at the same time. Her feet barely made a sound as she crept down the stairs.

"Hold him, Pete," she called softly.

Pete's response was two sharp barks—his joyful greetings. Still clutching the gun, she opened her front door.

Jim and Sleddog were toiling over the top of the ridge, carrying a large, unwieldy object. Hannah froze. Her emotions raged through her with gale force, and she clutched the front of her robe to still her shaking. His name formed on her lips, but she was speechless.

Jim looked up and saw her. In the eerie summer-light of near dawn, he stood at the top of the ridge and stared. Passion ripped through him so strongly, his knees actually became weak. Never taking his eyes off her, he dropped his end of the burden. "We'll deal with this later, Sleddog," he said quietly.

He took one step toward Hannah, cursing himself for waiting two weeks before coming to her. Damn his stiff-necked pride, he raged. He advanced slowly, savoring the moment, dragging out the anticipation until it zinged between them like the vibrations of a too-tight bowstring. A flush crept into her cheeks, the high coloring of desire.

When he was close enough to touch her, he stopped, his hands crammed firmly in his pockets. Their ragged breathing filled the air. "Hannah?"

"You came," she whispered.

"Yes." Still he didn't touch her.

"You shouldn't have."

"I'll always come. I'll follow you to the ends of the earth until you say yes."

Her hands trembled on the front of her robe, and her gun slid to the porch floor. "I can't . . . but . . . heaven help me . . ." She stopped speaking. With Jim beside her, reasons didn't matter anymore. Suddenly she reached for him.

That was all the sign he needed. He enfolded her close to his heart and buried his face in her hair. "Hannah, my love, my love," he said over and over.

Cupping her face, he dragged his lips over hers with agonizing slowness. Her body trembled.

"Ahh, yes."

He lifted his head. "Did you miss me, Hannah?"

She tangled her hands in his hair and pulled his head back down. "Please . . ."

Seeing Hannah's eyes smoky with desire and her hair tumbled from sleep, Jim lost his control. His mouth took hers with a fierceness that tried to deny anything between them except love. Hannah matched him, fire with fire.

Even Sleddog, who had lived close enough to nature to know a mating game when he saw it, became a little embarrassed. He cleared his throat loudly then, getting no response, he left his burden on the path and stomped up the front steps.

"I don't know about you," he practically shouted as he passed by them and stomped into the cabin, "but I'm starving. It's not every day a man gets up in the middle of the night to help deliver a bathtub."

Hannah broke away and looked up at Jim. "A bathtub?"

"The male of the species typically brings gifts when he comes courting."

She looked toward the path, and there it was, an antique bathtub, sitting in all its clawfooted splendor in the middle of her flower bed. She gave a hoot of joy, running toward the tub as she shouted.

"A tub? Jim! A tub!" She bent over and ran her hand around the cold porcelain rim. "It's heavenly. It's divine. It's absolutely stupendous."

He grinned. "I take it you like the present."

"Like it? I love it."

"Then marry me."

"Marry you?" Suddenly she became sober. "I've already told you no. I thought I made that very clear in San Francisco. I won't change my mind, Jim. I cannot accept this tub."

"The tub is my wedding gift to you."

"A wedding gift? You're trying to buy me with a tub?"

"It's the Indian way. I learned it from my friend Colter."

"He suggested a tub?"

"Well, not exactly. He suggested two mares and a stallion."

Hannah only had to look at the mischievous twinkle in Jim's eyes to know he was teasing. Serious or joking, it didn't matter, she thought. She loved all his moods. With a great effort she forced herself to be sensible.

"I won't take your gift, Jim. I won't do anything to give you false hope. It wouldn't be fair."

"If you won't take it, I guess I'll just have to abandon it out there for a birdbath. I'm sure as hell not hauling it back down that cliff. Anyway, what will we tell Sleddog? I got him out of bed this morning at two to help me deliver that wedding present."

"Don't keep calling it that."

"Well, call it an I'm-sorry-I-acted-such-an-ass gift."

"A what?"

"I'm-sorry—"

"No," she interrupted, laughing. "Please don't repeat it."

He took her hand and lifted it to his lips. "I'm sorry, Hannah . . . sorry I waited so long to come to you, sorry I didn't give you more preparation before I proposed, sorry I ever let you you leave San Francisco, sorry I didn't make you mine the first time I laid eyes on you in the cow pasture in Greenville."

"Jim." That's all she could bring herself to say. Just his name. But the way she said it made his heart leap. Her soft, jazzy voice wrapped the word in velvet and delivered it as a whole litany of love.

"I'm not leaving, Hannah. So you might as well let me and this tub in the door, or prepare to have us camp out here on your front porch."

Hannah swung her gaze back to the tub. It was the most unusual gift she'd ever heard of—and the most thoughtful. Of all the trappings of civilization she'd left behind, only the tub caused her regret and envy. How she'd missed the long, luxurious soaks she'd indulged in before she chose the primitive life! And how discerning of Jim to recognize the one material possession she longed for. It was as if he knew what was in her heart and soul.

She wanted the tub; she almost lusted for the tub. Could she accept the gift, she wondered, and still remain staunch against his marriage proposal? The porcelain gleamed at her in the early morning sun, and she fell madly in love. She absolutely could not resist those lovely old claw feet and that wonderful deep basin of pure pleasure.

"I'll take it." She turned back to face him. "Thank you. It's the best present I've ever received." Seeing the eager glow on his face, she sought to set him straight. "But, Jim, I make no promises."

"All I'm asking for is a hearing." He touched her hair briefly, just where the sunshine burnished it with fire. "The tub is yours, love. No strings attached."

They went inside and had breakfast with Sleddog.

Instead of resigning herself to Jim's presence, Hannah found that she had a hard time squelching her joy. In the end she decided to forget about why he had come and simply revel in the moment.

Her step was light as she went into the small bathroom to change into a shirt and a denim skirt. After she came out, the three of them hauled the antique bathtub into Hannah's cabin.

It was too big for the bathroom.

"Never mind. We'll put it here." Jim positioned it grandly to the left of the fireplace, just outside the small bathroom enclosure. "Who else do you know who can have a bubble bath beside a cozy fire?"

Hannah laughed. "It's perfect."

In honor of the new masterpiece, she canceled her day's work, and the three of them set about installing the tub. Of the three, Hannah was the handiest with tools, but none of them knew a thing about plumbing.

"It's a good thing I ain't hankering for one of these contraptions. Nature's good enough for me." Sleddog sat back on his haunches and viewed with disgust the pile of screwdrivers and hammers and nuts and bolts and copper tubing. "Yessir, a good dip in the crick every Saturday night ought to see a body through."

Jim rolled his eyes at Hannah, and they both suppressed their laughter.

"I think we can handle it from here, Sleddog." Jim pulled a roll of bills from his pocket.

"Keep yer money. If neighbors would be neighborly instead of expecting a reward every time they do a good deed, the rest of the world might be nigh as good as Alaska."

"You can come up and take a bubble bath sometime." Hannah smiled as she made the offer.

Sleddog looked horrified. "Me! In a tubful of bubbles. I'd as soon rassle with a walrus. Thank you just the same."

Hannah went with him back down the path and over the ridge to his pickup truck. Bending down, she planted a kiss on his shiny bald spot. "Thanks, Sleddog. You're a real friend."

"Ain't no need to thank me. From the looks of things, that young feller would have got up here with that tub if he'd had to strap it to his back and crawl. Reminds me of that old moose that raises hell around here every September when he comes bugling for a mate."

Chuckling, Hannah waved good-bye. Then she headed back to her cabin.

Jim was on his knees, struggling with a piece of copper tubing, addressing the tub in language that would do a sailor proud.

"I don't think that tub understands a word you've said."

When he turned around, Hannah laughed.

"What's so funny?"

"You should see your face; it's covered with grease."

"Oh, yeah? You think that's funny, do you?" He stood up and came toward her.

Hannah could have outdistanced him at any time, but she wanted to be caught. And she didn't dare think about that any further. When he hauled her against his chest, she circled her arms around him. It seemed the natural thing to do under the circumstances.

"Let's see if you think this is funny." Jim rubbed his nose against her cheek. "And this." He trailed a greasy hand down the side of her neck and into the top of her blouse.

At the lightest touch of his fingers, her breasts filled and her nipples tightened to hard points. Her eyes went languid as she reached down for his zipper. That, too, seemed the natural thing to do.

"It's not so funny," she whispered. "It's not funny at all." As she gazed into his eyes, she stopped thinking at all. Instinct took over.

For a long moment there was no sound in the cabin except their labored breathing, then Jim groaned.

With one movement he lifted her skirt and pulled down her panties. He took her standing up, her skirt bunched around her waist and her panties pooling around her ankles. It was hard and fast and frenzied. It was the coming together of two wild creatures whose only thought was to satisfy their raging need.

When it was over, he smoothed down her skirt and pulled her close. "I didn't mean to do it that way, Hannah."

And she knew that in one battle, at least, Jim had won, always would win. She might deny that she would be his wife until kingdom come, but from that moment on she would never turn away from his lovemaking. "Any way, any time." She pressed her face to his chest. "What are we going to do?"

His hands caressed her back and moved upward to tangle in her thick hair. "I'm going to spend the next two days convincing you to marry me."

"Only two days?"

"Yes. Next Monday I'll be back at my desk at *The Daily Spectator*, working like the devil to catch up. I managed to escape this weekend. Starting tonight, we'll have two days of heaven, Hannah."

"The two days of heaven started the minute you came over the ridge."

"That will do for starters, Dr. Donovan." He stepped back and smiled at her. "And now, what do you say we get to work on my wedding present."

It took them all day to install the tub.

"But we have no bubble bath," Hannah lamented when they had finished.

Triumphantly Jim unpacked his duffel bag and held a bottle aloft.

"Lavender." Hannah read the label. "What a luscious, old-fashioned fragrance."

"My mother's favorite."

Hannah put the bottle on the side of the tub. "Tell me more about her."

He straddled a chair beside the fireplace. "She loved lavender. We hardly had the price of a meal, much less an extravagance. There was a bath shop six blocks from our apartment, on the way to one of the houses she worked in."

Hannah watched his face as he talked. There was no bitterness there, no self-pity, merely an acceptance of the way things had been in his childhood.

"I used to meet her after work and walk her home. Always, she'd stop in front of the bath shop. 'Jim,' she'd say, 'lavender is the fragrance of real ladies.' Then she'd straighten her shoulders, and we'd walk on home."

He left the chair and began to pace the room. "When I was ten I had a paper route. I saved pennies for a year. I had just enough to buy her one of those little paper pillows filled with lavender. I'll never forget the look on her face that Christmas morning. You'd have thought I'd bought her a queen's crown."

The bottle of lavender bubble bath sitting on the edge of the tub took on a new significance for Hannah. It was no longer just a fragrance he had chosen; it was a bottle of memories, the sweet, sad memories of his childhood.

"Thank you, Jim," she said quietly.

Turning, he smiled. "For what?"

"For sharing a part of your past with me."

He crossed the room and took her in his arms. "I want to share my future with you too." His hands caressed her back. "Hannah, don't you see? We belong together. We met against all odds. Fate brought us together, and love will see us through."

"You can say that now, Jim. But what about later? What will you say when John Searles turns you loose again on the back streets and alleys of San Francisco? What will happen to our future when you take up your gauntlet and become the West Coast Warrior again?"

"I've never stopped being that warrior. I've merely been given a reprieve, a time to woo the woman I love"—he lifted a strand of her hair and brought it to his lips—"the woman I'll always love."

"Let's not talk; let's take a bubble bath."

He leaned back and lifted that sardonic brow at her. "Woman, I like your straightforward way of seduction. Nothing subtle, just get right to the point."

She gave him an arch smile. "Who said anything about seduction? I was merely offering to share my bath with you."

"I hope you're planning to make up for banning me from your bath in Greenville."

She laughed. "You'll never know how close I came to pulling you into the tub."

"You'll never know how close I came to getting in—whether you wanted me to or not."

Jim started toward the tub, but Hannah put a hand on his arm and stopped him. "Would you mind building a small fire?"

"I'll light your fire anytime, Hannah."

She smiled. "In the fireplace."

One look at her wicked, witty face told him that whatever she had in mind would add up to total delight. Without another word he started to build a fire.

Hannah turned off all the lights so that the cabin was lit only by the red-gold flicker of the fire and the misty summer-night glow that poured through the skylight. She led Jim to a chair beside the fire.

"I hope this is a ringside seat."

"The best in the house," she said as she walked toward the tub. Turning the hot water on full force, she dumped in the lavender. The steamy fragrance rose from the tub, permeating the cabin. With the water whooshing beside her, Hannah turned back to Jim. Ever so slowly she began to unbutton her blouse. His eyes glistened as a glimpse of white satin came into view. It was another of those delightfully feminine garments she wore under her functional work clothes, a tiny wisp of white satin and lace.

Jim's passion rose as he glimpsed her dark nipples through the white lace. What a woman, he thought. She could handle a hammer, a team of sled dogs, and a demanding career as easily as she could breathe. And yet she was as feminine as the white lace on her teddy. With one graceful gesture of her arm she lifted her heavy hair and arched her neck. The movement caused her nipples to break free of their lace restraints. They pointed provocatively at Jim, luscious and inviting.

He made a move to rise, but Hannah held up her hand. It was her show. He let her have it, even if the effort at control killed him.

Her thumbs hooked the waistband of her denim skirt. It slithered slowly down her hips, revealing the French-cut sides of her teddy. With her nipped-in waist, her long legs, and the delicious swelling of her hips, she was a delectable banquet waiting to be devoured.

With a smile designed to set every wolf in the wilderness to howling, Hannah leaned over the tub. The view presented to Jim sent his blood pressure up at least to stroke level, he calculated. Hannah turned back around, and with the languid look of a sorceress let a handful of the fragrant water trickle between her breasts. In the firelight the water turned to gold, hot molten gold. Her rosy nipples pouted at him through the wet material. Still smiling, she dipped another handful of water and sent it cascading across the flat planes of her stomach. The bright drops of moisture traveled slowly downward, licking Hannah as intimately as a lover. Wet satin and lace molded her body.

She repeated the process until she was sleek and glistening, then she started toward him, using that walk that made him want to lay kingdoms at her feet. She stood proudly before him, his smoke-and-fire woman, wet and ready, and gilded by the firelight.

There was no sound in the room except Jim's ragged breathing.

"Good Lord, woman, do you mean to drive me mad?"

She smiled. "Only for two days."

"I'll take what I can get." He reached for her. Pulling her close, he peeled away the teddy and licked the small drops of water that clung to her stomach. The warmth of the fire, the fragrance of lavender, and the nearness of Hannah filled his senses. "This could turn out to be the longest bath in the history of man," he said as his tongue followed the path of moisture.

It was a long time before they made it to the tub, and an even longer time in the tub. Among the fragrant bubbles they discovered pleasures they'd only dreamed of. Forgotten were the separations, the silences, the secret fears that kept them apart. Nothing mattered except the two of them and the great moments they shared.

Eleven

They had one night of wonder.

During that time they didn't talk much, merely pleasured themselves with each other. Their loving was so bright, so precious that they were both afraid talking would spoil it.

But the pressing matter of marriage remained on Jim's mind. At breakfast on the day after his arrival, he decided the time had come to broach the subject.

"Hannah. Let's talk."

"I'll make fresh coffee."

When she started to rise, he stopped her. Catching her hand, he pulled her gently back into her chair.

"Stay . . . please. I don't need fresh coffee; I need you."

She lifted her eyes toward the loft bed. "We could . . ."

"Hannah, you siren. If you keep tempting me, I'll never get around to another marriage proposal."

"That's the general idea." She turned her face away from his and gazed at the antique tub. She'd been gloriously happy until he mentioned marriage. Why couldn't things go on forever just the way they were? No commitment, no relinquishing of control, no possibility of failure.

"I love you, Hannah. I want us to be married, to have a life together, to have a family together."

She pulled her hand away. "Please don't touch me while you're saying those things. I can't think straight when you touch me."

"All right. Nothing physical." He settled back in his chair and pulled out his pipe. "You know, Colter was the first to discover that you were the woman I'd been searching for all my life. I had this impossible vision—a dream woman, someone old-fashioned and sweet and very dependent. All the time I was searching, my dream woman was right in front of my nose. You, Hannah."

Hannah sat very still, concentrating on his every word. She'd promised him a hearing, and she owed it to both of them to make it a fair one.

"Did that dream include a cozy house and lots of children?"

"Yes. It still does—maybe. At least, it includes the children." He swung his gaze around her cabin. "I've grown accustomed to this place. I can picture lace curtains at the windows and the two of us sitting beside the fire, sipping wine and making babies. Everything will work, Hannah, as long as I have you—my dream woman."

A homemaker, she thought. *He probably isn't even aware of it, but he wants to turn me into a homemaker.* She felt stifled. But she stilled her panic long enough to raise a sensible issue.

"But you've always done big-city work—crime fighting."

"While I was here doing those stories on your work, I felt a certain creative freedom that I hadn't felt in years. I've always known that someday I would do other kinds of writing. Now is the time to explore all the possibilities. We can work out a compromise, Hannah. We could work out a way to divide our time and our work between San Francisco and Glacier Bay."

"Who would give up the most time? Which one of us would leave his work behind? How much of your work in San Francisco would you give up for me?" His hesitation before he answered was slight, but she saw it.

"As long as I'm writing I'll be happy."

She jumped up and began to pace the room. "No! I won't let you. You'd be miserable."

"I wouldn't. I told you—"

"And then you'd grow to hate me." She whirled on him, interrupting him. "I won't give up my work for any man, and I won't ask that of you."

"Hannah," he said, reaching for her, but she side-stepped him. "I'm not asking you to give up your work."

"Aren't you?"

"No."

"Are you sure about that?"

"Positive."

"You called me your dream woman. You've assigned all your dreams to me. You say you've given up that image of a sweet, old-fashioned girl, and yet you envision the hearth fire and the lace curtains and the children." She stopped her pacing and faced him, hands on her hips. "Jim, you haven't given up that dream woman. You're merely trying to make me fit the mold."

"No. I love you the way you are."

"Independent, stubborn, opinionated . . ."

"Dedicated, generous, and very, very feminine."

"I won't do the lace-curtain bit."

"Forget the damned lace curtains." He jumped up from the table. Taking her by the shoulders, he forced her to look at him. "I love you, Hannah. And I mean to have you. It's as simple as that."

Hallie's first marriage played through Hannah's mind—Robert, domineering and demanding, and Hallie, losing her freedom. She wouldn't fall into the same trap as her twin sister. "No," she shouted. "No man can have me."

Jim's lips crushed down on hers. He hadn't meant to do it this way, he thought as he took the wild sweetness of her mouth; but what in the hell could a man do against the stubbornness of Dr. Hannah Donovan. He felt the swift yielding of her body, and his own rose to meet the challenge. As he slipped her robe from her shoulders, his last thought was that Hannah had been raising some legitimate questions, and he should be addressing them. But who could blame a man for being distracted by the wild, wanton pleasure of this fire-and-smoke woman?

Lifting her in his arms, he carried her to the hearth rug. Thoughts of marriage were pushed aside as they lost themselves in the age-old rhythms of love.

Jim's time in Glacier Bay seemed to be over before it had begun.

That's what Hannah was thinking as she stood in the small airport at Gustavus, waiting for Jim's flight to be called.

"I'll be back, Hannah." Jim slid his hand under her lightweight sweater and caressed her back. "Don't think I'm discouraged by your continued refusals. And don't ever think that I'll give up. I won't."

"It will be a losing battle, Jim. I've made up my mind and I won't change."

He smiled. "It seems to me you've said never before."

Her cheeks pinked. "That was different. Going to bed with a man one finds"—she paused, searching his face—"attractive is quite a different thing from marriage."

"Attractive? You find me attractive?"

She had only to look at the devilish twinkle in his eye to know she was being teased.

"You know what I mean."

"Why, Dr. Hannah Donovan. Is that a blush I see?"

Behind them the loudspeaker blared.

"Your fight's being called."

He cupped her face and leaned down for one last desperate kiss. "I love you, Hannah. I chased you out of habit, followed you out of intrigue, and fell in love with you out of the blue. And I won't let you go." He released her face and started for the gate. Turning, he called. "Remember that, Dr. Donovan. I love you."

She was oblivious to the smiling faces that turned in her direction. All she could think of was Jim Roman, the West Coast Warrior. He'd taken her by storm once more, and she wasn't sure she'd survived this invasion.

She walked to the window and watched until his plane became a mere speck in the sky, then she left the airport, climbed into her gray van, and headed back to her cabin.

For the next two days she wrestled with the loneliness and the feeling that she'd turned loose something precious. In spite of her turmoil, her work didn't suffer. Instead, she noticed the same sharp edge of awareness she'd had since Jim Roman came into her life. Strike another Rai episode, she thought. That part of her past became a closed chapter.

But it seemed to her that there were still insurmountable problems in her relationship with Jim. She couldn't be that simple dream woman he wanted. All she could do was bide her time.

It was the letters from Hallie and from San Francisco that set her into action.

Going through her mail at the institute on the Tuesday night after Jim had left, she came across Hallie's letter.

"Hannah," it said, "I know I promised that I would never lecture again, but you've been on my mind. A part of me feels your unease, and I don't know what's going on. You're never near the phone when I call. Is it love, Hannah? If so, please know this: Love is worth any risk and there is no problem that is too big to solve."

She laid aside Hallie's letter and went through the rest of her mail. There were the usual requests for her to give lectures, a few applications from marine biology graduates looking for work, and a letter from San Francisco. Hannah opened if first. It was a job offer.

For years there had been a difference of opinion in the scientific community about the benefits of keeping whales in captivity for study and later releasing them to the wild. Hannah always had been of the school that preferred studying them in the wild. Dr. Paley Overstreet, renowned cetologist from San Francisco, wanted her to do some work with whales in captivity. He hoped to create a crossover of scientists and perhaps a meeting of the minds on the question of captivity versus in-the-wild studies.

Hannah pondered Dr. Overstreet's offer for a long time. Like a counterpoint to a melody, the phrase love is worth any risk kept running through her mind. At last she flung the letters aside and started back toward her cabin.

Pete was waiting for her on the trail. Summer will be over soon, Hannah thought as they made their way through the misty evening light. When her cabin came into view, she thought of spending another winter there. For the first time since she'd come to Glacier Bay, the thought brought no thrill. She'd have the Yukon Quest, of course, and her work was always exciting but something would be missing.

Suddenly Hannah knew what that something was: love. She'd accepted Jim as a challenge, seduced him out of curiosity, and fallen in love with him out of need. Yes, she finally admitted to herself, need. She needed Jim Roman, and there was only one thing to do about it—take the risk.

Her steps quickened as she neared her front porch. She had problems to solve and plans to make. She'd always been very good at those two things. And now, she thought, she was going to excel.

Hannah was up far into the night thinking through her problems with Jim, and she stayed home Wednesday to carry out her plans. She'd just completed her call to San Francisco when she heard a knock at her door. Sleddog was standing on the front porch, his tufted white hair pomaded and looking like shiny Ping-Pong balls on his head. He was wearing his Sunday-best shirt and his new coveralls. And he was looking as uncomfortable as a sinner in a church full of saints.

"Sleddog!" Hannah greeted him with genuine pleasure. "Come in."

"Well, I didn't mean to bother you." Sleddog stood just inside the door and cast his eyes in the direction of the tub. "It's just that . . . well, I thought . . . you see . . ." He finally gave up. Closing his mouth, he rocked back on his worn boot heels and looked as if he wanted to be anywhere but where he was.

Sleddog was usually taciturn, but he'd never been so obviously ill at ease. Hannah almost panicked. Was he bringing bad news about Jim? Surely somebody would have called her. She reached out and clutched his arm.

"Is it Jim? Has something bad happened to him?"

"Lordy, no." In the face of her panic, Sleddog relaxed. "It's just that . . ." He gave the tub one last look, then rushed forward like a snowball down a mountain, gaining momentum as he talked. "Well, you know, you said something about me using that new-fangled tub whenever I wanted to, and well, it's like this, I'm gittin' a mite old for the crick. Them cold waters chill my bones. And well, I was wonderin'. . ."

"Of course." Hannah's relief was so great, she practically dragged him across the floor toward the tub. "I'll turn on the water and you can take all the time you like. I need to take the dogs on a run anyhow." She turned the hot water on full force. "Do you want bubbles?"

Sleddog's face colored. "Since I'm being an old fool anyhow, I might as well go all the way."

Hannah dumped in a generous amount of lavender. Sleddog sniffed deeply.

"Ain't that a pretty smell? Reminds me of my grandmother."

"You just take your time, Sleddog. I'll give a yell when I come back."

Hannah turned off the water, reached for her sweater, and left him with his bubble bath. By the time she'd reached the front porch, Sleddog had stripped and was up to his neck in lavender bubbles. He was having the time of his life.

Hannah could hear him singing all the way out to the kennels. She smiled. Life was full of unexpected joy, she decided. Had it always been, or had she just never taken the time to notice until she fell in love with Jim?

She raced her dogs down the trail, singing.

Thursday hadn't been a day off after all.

Jim wasn't sorry. Actually he'd been glad for the work. It had kept his mind off Hannah. Four days away from her had felt like an eternity.

Thank heaven his work left him no time for useless soul searching. The business with the drug ring had suddenly come to a head. Jim's reappearance at the newspaper had drawn the dealers out of hiding. Using some of his tips and the leads they'd been building for months, the police finally had rounded up the kingpin. He'd turned out to be a low-profile businessman whose company was a front for the ring. No mob connections, nothing international, merely a local gangster with plans to expand all along the West Coast.

He stepped aboard his houseboat, peeling off his shirt as he went. It had been a hectic day, and he could use a beer, he decided. Tossing his shirt across the railing, he headed below deck. He heard the sound the minute his foot was on the ladder. It was a strange, soft, eerie noise that made the back of his neck prickle. Jim froze. An extra burst of adrenaline flowed through him, and all his muscles tensed for action. Getting into a half crouch, he leaned cautiously down and peered into his living quarters.

Hannah was perched on the side of his bed.

"Great merciful heaven!" His mouth dropped open, and he could do nothing but stare.

She was wearing a diaphanous gown that made him think of angels. Except there was nothing angelic about Dr. Hannah Donovan. In that dress she was pure bombshell, one hundred percent vamp, and all woman.

"Hello, Jim." She rose from the bed and stood, facing him and smiling. Backlit by the afternoon sun coming through the open portholes, she was stunningly, gloriously naked under the gauzy gown. All his dreams paled in comparison to the reality of Hannah. "What took you so long?" When she spoke in that blues-music voice of hers, he felt as if he'd been stripped and caressed with velvet.

He clung foolishly to the top of the ladder, scarcely able to believe what he was seeing and hearing. "A little cleanup job at the newspaper."

"How is it going now that you're back?"

"My return to the paper set things in motion. The police rounded up the drug ring."

Hannah drew a long breath. "It's over, then?"

"Until something else comes along."

Neither of them moved. Hannah still hung back beside the bed and Jim still hovered on the ladder. Both of them seemed reluctant to disturb the currents that were flowing between them.

Finally, when the silence had stretched so thin the air seemed to vibrate, Hannah spoke. "I'm so glad you're safe."

"Thank you."

The shock of seeing her in his houseboat was beginning to wear off. But not the excitement. Never the excitement, he thought.

For the first time since he'd come below, Jim became aware of his surroundings. The weird sounds he'd heard were coming from his tape deck. He recognized them as Hannah's whale songs.

Strung across his portholes were lace curtains. Actual, honest-to-goodness lace curtains, he realized. He felt lightheaded with joy. Slowly he descended the ladder, never taking his eyes off Hannah.

"You brought your own music, I see."

"Yes. The song of the humpback whale. Recognize it?"

"Is that the same song that drove me from my sleeping bag?"

"No. This one is their mating song."

"Mating song?" he leaned against the ladder, careful not to let his exultation show on his face. Hannah had come to him. He thought he knew why, but he had to be very sure. Marriage was a lifetime commitment. This time he couldn't afford to let passion get in the way of understanding.

"Yes. Traditionally, when the whale seeks his mate, he courts her with his haunting love song."

"Are you courting me, Hannah?"

"Yes."

"Why?"

"I'm seeking you as a mate."

"A playmate?"

"No. A lifetime mate."

His heart thumped so loudly, he thought she surely could hear it, but he kept his careful distance.

"Marriage?"

"Yes. If you still want me."

He had to ram his fists into his pants pockets to keep from rushing across the room and sweeping her into his arms. There were many issues between them that had to be settled. And he realized that his first mistake had been in doing all the talking. No wonder Hannah had thought he wanted her to be his dream woman. He'd never given her a chance to say what was on her mind. He'd restrain his impatience to possess her even if the effort cost him an ulcer.

"I still want you, Hannah. Now and always."

She heaved a great sigh. Whether it was relief or contentment or merely nervousness, he didn't know.

"I've come to you. I even bought lace curtains." She gave him a rueful grin. "I never knew those things came in so many different sizes. Do they teach courses somewhere in dealing with lace curtains?"

"Are you planning to take a few, Hannah?"

"No, Jim. These curtains are merely symbolic. I don't plan to embrace the domestic scene." She lifted her chin in an unconscious gesture of defiance. "If you want me, you'll have to take me just the way I am."

"Hannah . . ." Jim started to reach for her, then stopped himself. Ramming his hands into his pockets, he continued. "The woman I thought I wanted probably would bore me to hell in two weeks time. You're brilliant and untamed and unpredictable and exciting. And I wouldn't have you any other way." He came across his pipe in the depths of his pocket and drew it out. He never took his eyes off Hannah as he tamped in tobacco and lit the pipe. "I want to marry you, Hannah, but not on my terms alone. We'll work that out together."

"I want it all, Jim. A career, a cottage, a cozy fire, even the damned lace curtains if somebody else will iron them."

"I wield a pretty fair iron."

She started to take a step toward him, then moved back. Her elegant blue eyes held his as she spoke. "I want children."

"Children?" Jim didn't know this was one of the things he'd been waiting to hear her say until she said it. He hadn't been sure she'd want a family. He'd even been prepared to give it up for her.

"Yes. I see no reason not to have children as well as a career. Other women do."

His heart sang. But still caution held him back.

He took a steadying puff on his pipe. "Where will your career be, Hannah? Glacier Bay?"

"Partially. You mentioned compromise."

"I did—and I meant it."

"I have an offer to work in San Francisco, studying whales in captivity. I could do that in the winter months and spend my summers at the institute in Glacier Bay."

"You're sure?"

She smiled. "So sure," she said, "that I'm already setting up interviews with graduate students to assist Sol in Glacier Bay this winter. So certain, that I've already accepted the offer of the San Francisco Leviathan Foundation to work with them on a seasonal basis." She walked slowly toward him. "I want it all, Jim. And I've made up my mind to have it."

The sheer gown swirled so that she seemed to float toward him. When she was close enough to touch, she placed her palms on his bare chest. Her fragrance wafted over him. Lavender.

He sucked in his breath as her hands moved in sensuous circles. "We'll have it all." He tamped out his pipe and put it on a nearby table. "And I think now would be a good time to start. Don't you, Dr. Donovan?"

"If you hadn't said that, I was going to get my gun."

He caught her hands and pressed them over his heart. "You're packing iron?"

"You never can tell. I was prepared for a shotgun wedding." She leaned down to put her tongue on the pulse spot at the base of his throat.

"Will you settle for the old-fashioned kind with a preacher and our families present?" His hands bracketed her shoulders, and ever so slowly he slipped the gauzy gown downward.

"Could we talk about the wedding later?" She tangled her hands into his hair and drew him to her.

"Much later," he said.

They decided to have the wedding in Greenville.

At the end of the summer the entire Donovan clan gathered once more to see one of their own properly married. Mary Roman, John Searles, and Colter Gray Wolf made up the San Francisco contingent, and Sleddog came from Glacier Bay. It was the first time he'd ever been out of Alaska.

For Mary Roman and Anna Donovan, it was more than a wedding between their children, it was a reunion.

As they stood in the dressing room, waiting their turn to be called out and escorted down the aisle, they talked.

"I never dreamed my Jim would marry one of your children." Mary caught Anna's hands. "It's too good to be true."

"That Hannah is marrying at all is a miracle to me." Anna Donovan, looking almost as young and pretty as one of her daughters, smiled at her old friend. "I guess it took a man like your Jim to sweep her off her feet."

"Oh, my." Mary put her hand over her fluttering heart. "Just to think—you and I will be sharing grandchildren. That is—" She hesitated, remembering that her future daughter-in-law was a career woman, *Dr.* Hannah Donovan. "Do you think they'll have children?"

Anna laughed. "I'll tell you a secret, Mary. The Donovans are a fertile and prolific clan. We'll take turns baby-sitting." She reached up and adjusted her frothy lace hat. "I think they're calling for us."

While Mary and Anna were walking out together Hallie and Hannah were sharing a last heart-to-heart talk in the bride's dressing room.

"I'm so happy for you, Hannah." Hallie reached up and adjusted her sister's veil, the same veil she'd worn only a few months earlier.

"I'm a little bit scared." Hannah reached for her sister's hand. "Isn't that foolish? You'd think anybody who could face down a bull moose the way I did in that last Yukon Quest wouldn't be afraid of the devil."

"A husband hardly can be compared to a bull moose." Hallie grinned. "But then again . . ."

"Oh, stop your teasing." Hannah sucked in her breath and smoothed the Victorian wedding gown over her stomach. "It's snug. do I look all right?"

"Gorgeous."

"Is that the Wedding March?"

"Not yet. It's not time." Hallie picked up the bouquet that lay on a nearby table and handed it to her sister. "I know this is bad timing, but I just have to share my news with you. I've been bursting to tell someone."

Hannah took the bouquet. "What?"

"I'm pregnant." Seeing Hannah's shocked look, she grinned. "We're ecstatic. Of course, I know how you always caution me to plan everything, but sometimes wonderful things just happen."

Hannah clutched her bouquet so hard, she was sure she'd break the stems off. Hallie, pregnant.

They'd had mumps, measles, chicken pox, and flu together. In a short while they'd have been married in the same dress, in the same church. How long had it been? She thought back over the summer, the long, loving sessions with Jim that just had seemed to happen. She'd been so busy and happy, she hadn't planned, hadn't bothered to keep track. Good Lord, could it be? Could *she* be?

"Aren't you going to congratulate me?"

"Congratulations." Twins, Hannah thought. Why did everything always happen to them at the same time?

Hallie grabbed her hand. "Come on, Hannah. They're playing the Wedding March."

Hannah stood tall and proud. First things first, she decided. Right now she was getting married. Jim was waiting for her, and that's all she would think about.

Down at the altar rail, Jim looked up. Hannah filled his vision. Her hair tumbled over the white wedding gown like a bolt of black silk; her face was vivid and smiling, and her eyes were bright with promise. His dream woman. The woman he'd set out to capture and had ended up being her captive. His wildcat, his Hannah, his love. She floated toward him like a dream, but he knew she was real. He would never mistake Dr. Hannah Donovan—soon to be Roman—for anything except a flesh-and-blood woman.

Hannah looked deep into his eyes, and he saw his own love and commitment reflected there. He reached out his hand, and there in her family church, they exchanged the vows they'd written.

"I, Jim, take you, Hannah, to be my wife. Today

and in all the days to come I will love and cherish you, care for and keep you. Your celebrations will be my celebrations, your pain will be my pain, your joy, my joy—from this day to eternity."

"I, Hannah, take you, Jim, to be my husband. 'Whither thou goest, I will go, whither thou lodgest, I will lodge. They people shall be my people, and thy God my God.' "

Jim was awestruck as the most independent woman in the world pledged the age-old biblical vows of Ruth.

Hannah squeezed his hand. "Together we will face whatever life brings—with courage and with love." The minister added his blessing, and the West Coast Warrior leaned down to claim his bride with a kiss.

THE EDITOR'S CORNER

I feel envious of you. I wish I could look forward to reading next month's LOVESWEPTs for the first time! How I would love to sit back on a succession of the fine spring days coming up and read these six novels. They are just great and were loads of fun for us here to work on.

Starting off not with a bang but an *explosion*, we have the first novel in *The Pearls of Sharah* trilogy, **LEAH'S STORY**, LOVESWEPT #330, by Fayrene Preston. When Zarah, an old gypsy woman, gave her the wondrous string of creamy pearls, promising that a man with cinnamon-colored hair would enter her life and magic would follow, Leah insisted she didn't believe in such pretty illusions. But when handsome Stephen Tanner appeared that night at the carnival, she saw her destiny in his dark eyes and fiery hair. He found her fascinating, beautiful, an enchantress whose gypsy lips had never known passion until the fire of his kisses made her tremble and their sweetness made her melt. Leah had never fit in anywhere but with the gypsies, and she feared Stephen would abandon her as her parents had. Could he teach her she was worthy of his love, that the magic was in her, not the mysterious pearls? Do remember that this marvelous book is also available in hardcover from Doubleday.

Unforgettable Rylan Quaid and Maggie McSwain, that fantastic couple you met in **RUMOR HAS IT,** get their own love story next month in Tami Hoag's **MAN OF HER DREAMS**, LOVESWEPT #331. When Rylan proposes to Maggie at his sister's wedding, joy and fierce disappointment war in her heart. She has loved him forever, wants him desperately. But could he really be such a clod that he would suggest it was time he settled down, and she might as well be the one he did it with? Maggie has to loosen the reins he holds on his passion, teach Ry that he has love to give—and that she is the one great love of his life. Ry figures he's going to win the darling Maggie by showing he's immune to her sizzling charms. . . . This is a love story as heartwarming as it is hot!

From first to last you'll be breathless with laughter and a tear or two as you revel in Joan Elliott Pickart's **HOLLY'S**

(continued)

HOPE, LOVESWEPT #332. Holly Chambers was so beautiful . . . but she appeared to be dead! Justin Hope, shocked at the sight of bodies lying everywhere, couldn't imagine what disaster had befallen the pretty Wisconsin town or how he could help the lovely woman lying so pale and limp on the grass. When mouth-to-mouth resuscitation turned into a kiss full of yearning and heat, Justin felt his spirits soar. He stayed in town and his relationship with Holly only crackled more and warmed more with each passing day. But he called the world his oyster, while Holly led a safe life in her little hometown. Was love powerful enough to change Justin's dreams and to transform Holly, who had stopped believing in happily-ever-after? The answer is pure delight.

Next, we have the thrilling **FIRE AND ICE,** LOVESWEPT #333, from the pen—oops—word processor of talented Patt Bucheister. Lauren McLean may look serene, even ice-princess reserved, but on the inside she is full of fiery passion for John Zachary, her boss, her unrequited love . . . the man who has scarcely noticed her during the two or three years she has worked for him. When John unexpectedly gains custody of his young daughter, it is Lauren to the rescue of the adorable child as well as the beleaguered (and adorable!) father. Starved for ecstasy, Lauren wants John more than her next breath . . . and he is wild about her. But she knows far too much about the pain of losing the people she's become attached to. When John melts the icy barriers that keep Lauren remote, the outpouring of passion's fire will have you turning the pages as if they might scorch your fingers.

There's real truth-in-titling in Barbara Boswell's **SIMPLY IRRESISTIBLE,** LOVESWEPT #334, because it *is* a simply irresistibly marvelous romance. I'm sure you really won't be able to put it down. Surgeon Jason Fletcher, the hospital heartbreaker to whom Barbara has previously introduced you, is a gorgeously virile playboy with no scruples . . . until he steps in to protect Laura Novak from a hotshot young doctor. Suddenly Jason—the man who has always prided himself on not having a possessive bone in his body—feels jealous and protective of Laura. Laura's pulse races with excitement when he claims her, but when a near accident shatters her com-
(continued)

posure and forces long-buried emotions to the surface, grief and fury are transformed into wild passion. Danger lurks for Jason in Laura's surrender though, because she is the first woman he has wanted to keep close. And he grows desperate to keep his distance! Jason has always got what he wanted, but Laura has to make him admit he wishes for love.

We close out our remarkable month with one of the most poignant romances we've published, **MERMAID, LOVESWEPT #335**, by Judy Gill. In my judgment this story ranks right up there with Dorothy Garlock's beautiful **A LOVE FOR ALL TIME**, LOVESWEPT #6. Mark Forsythe knew it was impossible, an illusion—he'd caught a golden-haired mermaid on his fishing line! But Gillian Lockstead was deliciously real, a woman of sweet mystery who filled him with a joy he'd forgotten existed. When Gillian gazed up at her handsome rescuer, she sensed he was a man worth waiting for; when Mark kissed her, she was truly caught—and he was enchanted by the magic in her sea-green eyes. Both had children they were raising alone, both had lost spouses to tragedy. Even at first meeting, however, Gillian and Mark felt an unspoken kinship . . . and a potent desire that produced fireworks, and dreams shared. Gillian wanted Mark's love, but could she trust Mark with the truth and shed her mermaid's costume for the sanctuary of his arms? The answer to that question is so touching, so loving that it will make you feel wonderful for a long time to come.

Do let us hear from you!

Warm regards,

Carolyn Nichols

Carolyn Nichols
Editor
LOVESWEPT
Bantam Books
666 Fifth Avenue
New York, NY 10103